ROBERT DESNOS

# 𝕿HE 𝕻UNISHMENTS
# OF 𝕳ELL,
# OR 𝕹EW 𝕳EBRIDES

Frontispiece by Francis Picabia

Translated, and with a preface, by Natasha Lehrer
Verse translation by Chris Allen
Introduction by Marie-Claire Dumas

ATLAS PRESS, LONDON

Published by Atlas Press,
27 Old Gloucester St., London WC1N 3XX
©Éditions Gallimard, 1978
Frontispiece by Francis Picabia ©ADAGP, Paris and DACS, London 2017
Translation ©2017, Natasha Lehrer
Translation (verse) ©2017, Chris Allen
This edition ©2017, Atlas Press *bis*
All rights reserved.
Printed by CPI
A CIP record for this book is available from
The British Library.
ISBN: 978-0-9931487-3-6

# Contents

We are extremely grateful to
Olivia and Robert Temple
of the
Montparnasse Cultural Foundation
for funding the translation of this book.

THE PUNISHMENTS OF HELL

*Eclectics & Heteroclites* 18

Robert Desnos was born in Paris on 4 July 1900, the son of a market-trader at Les Halles who had ambitions for his son to continue his studies and go into business. The young Desnos resisted his father's bourgeois aspirations, and left school at sixteen without any qualifications. Any academic shortcomings were easily outweighed by the fact that he had long been a voracious reader of all genres, from popular serialised novels to Apollinaire, Rimbaud and Baudelaire, all of whose influences can be detected in his work. Alongside his vast knowledge of literature he was passionate about cinema, and began publishing poetry while he was still a teenager.

After fulfilling part of his compulsory military service in Morocco, Desnos returned to Paris in 1921, where he engineered an introduction to André Breton through Benjamin Péret, a friend of fellow poet and acquaintance Louis de Gonzague-Frick. He was soon attending meetings with the Surrealists and joining in their activities. In 1922, Breton, Desnos and several of the other writers in the group began to experiment with "sleeping-fits", or "*sommeils*", at which Desnos particularly excelled. Using techniques borrowed from spiritualism, these proto-Surrealists were not interested in any kind of communion between the living and the dead but rather in tapping the creative forces of the unconscious by means of "automatic" writing. Desnos and René Crevel seemed instinctively able to harness this direct and unmediated source of creativity that was a marker of early Surrealism. In 1922 Desnos also published his first book, a collection of Surrealistic aphorisms, created during his earliest experiments with "sleeping-fits", whose title was borrowed from Marcel Duchamp's pseudonym, *Rrose Sélavy.*

Although several years younger than the other Surrealists, Desnos was soon central to the group's research. Aragon described Desnos's almost uncanny ability to enter a trance-like state at will:

> In a café, amid all the voices, the bright lights, and the bustle, Robert Desnos need only close his eyes, and he talks, and among the books, the saucers, the whole ocean collapses with its prophetic racket, its vapours decorated with long oriflammes. However little he is encouraged by those who interrogate him, prophesy, the tone of magic, of revelation, of the French Revolution, the tone of the fanatic and the apostle, immediately follow. Under other conditions, Desnos, were he to maintain this delirium, would become the leader of a religion, the founder of a city, the tribune of a people in revolt.[1]

When Breton came to write the *Surrealist Manifesto* in 1924, he in turn eulogised the young writer. Desnos, he wrote, has "perhaps got closest to the Surrealist truth." Breton went on,

> … in the course of the numerous experiments he has been a party

8

to, [Desnos] has fully justified the hope I placed in Surrealism and leads me to believe that a great deal more will still come of it. Desnos *speaks Surrealist* at will. His extraordinary agility in orally following his thought is worth as much to us as any number of splendid speeches which are lost, Desnos having better things to do than record them. He reads himself like an open book, and does nothing to retain the pages, which fly away in the windy wake of his life.[2]

Desnos's automatic writing sessions "produced texts that seemed to hover somewhere between sense and non-sense, the significant and the insignificant, the ordinary and the extraordinary, the prophetic and the mundane".[3] His novella, *The Punishments of Hell, or New Hebrides*, written in 1922 though it remained unpublished for over half a century, was one of several works passed around the Surrealists in manuscript form.

Desnos acknowledged as one of the two main literary influences for *The Punishments of Hell* the 1920 text *The Magnetic Fields*, by Breton and Philippe Soupault. This was the first text produced through automatic writing during the Dada period and was only later canonised as the first Surrealist text. Inspired by the automatic writing that had produced *The Magnetic Fields*, Desnos used the technique to compose something resembling a sequential narrative. (This narrative component would become more pronounced in *Mourning for Mourning* and *Liberty or Love!*) *The Punishments of Hell*, with its distinct Dadaist qualities (particularly the almost meaningless verse in a style reminiscent of Tristan Tzara) and what would become the signature style of Surrealism (dreams, the marvellous, extreme lyricism), can be seen as one of the first of the movement's texts to show a route out from the aggression of Dada towards something more optimistic, though it is shot through by frequent scenes of violence and cruelty.

As Marie-Claire Dumas explains in her introduction to the 2016 Gallimard edition which follows, there is no definitive version of Desnos's novella, and even the title is protean: in the two existing manuscripts it is variously called *New Hebrides* or *The Punishments of Hell*. It is worth drawing attention here to the double meaning of *"nouvelles"* in the French title *"Nouvelles Hébrides"*, which can mean both "new" and "short stories", though the latter sense is only revealed in the play on words of a title that Desnos appears to have briefly considered but then rejected (perhaps for being too obvious), *Nouvelles Hybrides*, which can be read as "hybrid stories". The novel, with its blending of elements of both Dada and Surrealism, is indeed a text created out of hybrid influences.

Automatic writing, with its links to psychoanalysis, offered Desnos and others who experimented with it a way of exploring their unconscious impulses and desires without necessarily taking responsibility for them, since they apparently came forth from the unconscious mind without rational mediation. A strikingly perverse eroticism and sexual violence pervades the text from beginning to end, alongside other themes dear to both Dadaists and Surrealists that recur throughout.

The narrative culminates in the cemetery that commemorates those who lost their lives in the sinking of the frigate *La Sémillante*. Desnos was, as Robert McNab reminds us, "fascinated by the sea, by steamships, shipwrecks and ocean travel";[4] Aragon described him as having "strange ships in every fold of his brain",[5] and of course travel was central to the Surrealist adventure, the idea of discovering uncharted lands a perfect metaphor for the *aventure mentale*, the forays into a dream world that stood at the centre of their artistic quest. In his cemetery Desnos buries a roster of famous characters, including admired revolutionaries such as Robespierre and Saint-Just, and a good number of his friends, who although somewhat notorious by then, were yet to achieve the fame that many would subsequently acquire. The cemetery could simultaneously be taken to represent, as Simon Baker suggests, the creation of an alternative literary pantheon — or perhaps its very opposite: the ironic "murder" of Desnos's friends and those who influenced him, a Dadaist wiping-clean of the slate of history. If one of the avowed ambitions of Dadaism was the elimination of the canonical heritage in the service of an absolute modernity,[6] then Surrealism would in turn replace it with an entirely new canon, which would include many of the corpses here.

The ironies have continued to multiply: after his death, Desnos himself was to become a beloved and, yes, canonical French poet, albeit not so much for his Surrealist writings. As for *The Punishments of Hell, or New Hebrides*, the novel would not be published until 1974, nearly 30 years after its author's death, with illustrations by Joan Miró. The two had first discussed a possible collaboration on a *"livre d'artiste"*, based on the manuscript, half a century earlier, but for various reasons it did not happen during the writer's lifetime. Desnos, an active member of the Resistance, was arrested by the Gestapo in Paris in February 1944 and sent eventually to the concentration camp of Theresienstadt in April 1945. He died there of typhus on 8 June, one month to the day after the war in Europe ended.

Natasha Lehrer

1. Louis Aragon, *A Wave of Dreams* (1924), trans. Adam Cornford. Available online at Duration Press.
2. Trans. Richard Seaver and Helen R. Lane, University of Michigan Press, 1969.
3. "The Period of the Sleeping Fits", by Eugene Thacker, *Metamute* (16 October 2013).
4. *Ghost Ships: A Surrealist Love Triangle*, New Haven and London: Yale University Press, 2004, p.107.
5. *Ibid.*
6. *Surrealism, History and Revolution*, Oxford: Peter Lang, 2007, pp.137–41.

# INTRODUCTION

In a letter dated 22 October 1922, which accompanied the manuscript of *New Hebrides* he was sending to Jacques Doucet,[1] Robert Desnos described the attached text as "my first work of prose, and I wrote it with no other purpose than to amuse myself, eager as I was to fill the void in which I found myself at the beginning of the year." According to a note on the manuscript, the text was written during April and May 1922.

Since childhood Desnos had enjoyed inventing stories and noting down his dreams, and in his introduction to the 139 pages he sent to Doucet, he said, "I have enjoyed making up [stories] for as long as I can remember", adding that they "fill my hours of solitude, usually before I fall asleep, lingering on into my dreams and serving as a sort of preface to them". *New Hebrides* does not appear to break with its author's commitment to a kind of writing that was straightforward and unpolished, unburdened with stylistic concerns, and whose sole stated purpose was his own amusement.

Still, Desnos soon discovered the urge to share his personal jottings and have them published, as is clear from a letter dated 20 July 1922 in which he thanked Francis Picabia for the "beautiful sketch" he had done to accompany the future publication. He also had a subscription form printed up for a "novel" to be entitled *The Punishments of Hell, or New Hebrides*. Soon after, the September 1922 issue of the magazine *Littérature* announced the book in its list of forthcoming publications, and presented the first pages of the novel under the title *The Punishments of Hell.* That is as far as it got to actually being published, however, and in fact, was *New Hebrides* "unpublishable"? In 1923 Louis Aragon suggested as much, in a letter to Doucet headed "A Year in Novels (July 1922 – August 1923)": "I can think of two novels, one by Benjamin Péret, the other by Robert Desnos, which will never find a publisher. They contain that shadowy power which has no influence in this world; they are the violent imaginings of two men who have not designed their gestures to match the conventional salon *décor.* It is possible that one day someone will discover *Death to the Pigs*[2] and *New Hebrides.* But perhaps not." Despite this, in 1924 André Breton still seemed to believe the Desnos might be published one day, referring in the first *Manifesto of Surrealism* to the "as yet unpublished works" *New Hebrides, Formal Disorder* and *Mourning for Mourning.* In fact, only the last of these three would be published during this period.

When *New Hebrides* was eventually published in 1978, in the version held in the Doucet archive, it was believed that another manuscript also existed, which had been the source of the extracts published in *Littérature,* though no one knew its whereabouts. This second manuscript was eventually located by Michel Murat in the possession of the publisher José Corti, to whom Desnos appears to have sent it in 1926. It was inevitable that the two manuscripts would be compared, and in 1985 Murat did so in a detailed article in *Pleine Marge* entitled *"The Punishments of Hell,* or the House of Correction". To indicate which version is being discussed in what follows, they will be referred to as either the "Doucet manuscript" or the "Corti manuscript".

It is worth pausing for a moment to reflect on the different titles under which the book has appeared. *The Punishments of Hell* is the title marked at the beginning of the Corti manuscript, as well as that of the extract published in *Littérature*. *New Hebrides* appears, however, from the letter he wrote to Doucet, to have been Desnos's preference, and this was the title given in the announcement of forthcoming publications in *Littérature*. It should be noted that Desnos avoided making the choice between the two in his subscription form for the "novel", according to which the title is *The Punishments of Hell, or New Hebrides.*

If the significance of this double title is considered in relation to the work itself, it is tempting to conclude that it was merely an arbitrary choice; however, although the two alternatives seem random, certain subtexts are clearly implied. As regards *The Punishments of Hell*, beyond the possible allusion to the special department of the same name in the Bibliothèque Nationale[3] where Desnos worked as secretary to Jean de Bonnefon, the more interesting suggestion has been made that this title may allude to a work published by the jurist Joseph Ortolan in 1873, *Dante's Punishments of Hell.* While Desnos doesn't seem to have had any interest in the contents of the book, he may well have decided to appropriate its title, as can be seen by his somewhat abstruse reference in the subscription form to the "young *comingman*[4] of the Cour d'Assises" (in other words, a young jurist aspiring to work in the Cour d'Assises, or Assize Court). As for the title *New Hebrides*, on page 9 of the Doucet manuscript there is an inspired play on words: "It was he [the Captain] who brought me back my hat after the wind had carried it all the way to the New Hybrides." This slippage of a single letter was corrected when the extract was published in *Littérature*, and it seems to be quite clear from the many other mentions in the text that Desnos did indeed intend it to be *Hebrides* and not *Hybrides*. In the text's geography, which is traversed in all directions by the author's fantasies, different islands appear and reappear throughout: on the very first page we encounter Zanzibar, a "desert island", then there are the New Hebrides, which welcome the escaped hat, there is "a little island" chosen by Miss Flowers, the Captain and Louis Morin for their erotic frolics, and finally the Iles Sanguinaires off the coast of Corsica, which Desnos designated as the site where the frigate *Sémillante* sank,[5] a place given over to death.

Desnos decided, perhaps in a spirit of defiance, to call this collection of short stories, written for his own pleasure in idle moments, a "novel". Was this a trick to deceive his readers, or was it more the desire to place himself, like Aragon, within the controversial field of narrative writing produced by the group associated with *Littérature*? To confuse things further, the Corti manuscript is divided into chapters in the traditional way, whilst the Doucet manuscript keeps the individual texts separate, clearly distinct from one another both in terms of when each was written and in terms of the different handwriting, ink and types of paper used. The structured unity of the 10 chapters in the Corti manuscript is thus contrasted with the relatively disparate nature of the 22 fragments in the Doucet manuscript. In his comparison of the two manuscripts, Murat kept close track of the changes Desnos made from one version to the next. The individual stories retain their form, while little has been cut apart from the odd verse stanza, and there are only a few additions. Even so, these small changes are often quite apparent. Transitions between episodes have been neatened up, a basic minimum of punctuation has been inserted, verb tenses have been made consistent and word choices improved. But none of the *hybrid* nature has been edited out of the *novel*, which moves between narratives recounted at breakneck speed, versified passages that spout forth from the "singing tap" (see page @24), impassioned speeches, ridiculous conversations and brief dramatic scenes. Nevertheless, from the first to the final draft of this "Surrealist composition", a single breath carries along both words and images right up until the explosion of the final syllable, "Ping!", in which the scriptural energy of the tale finds both its apotheosis and its destruction.

## *The Influence of* The Poet Assassinated *and* The Magnetic Fields

In his letter to Doucet dated 22 October 1922,[6] Desnos stated that: "I think in the main I have been influenced by *The Poet Assassinated*, and, for the supernaturalistic part, *The Magnetic Fields*." The influence of *The Magnetic Fields* (1920), which can certainly be seen as the starting point of this Surrealist adventure, is very obvious, specifically in the way that Breton's text follows the principle by which the flow of automatic writing is generated, where words are written down as they come to mind, with no attempt at any rational control or literary finesse. Desnos discovered in this foundational text the validation he dreamed of, the freedom to commit himself fully to the thrill of the interior monologue that was second nature to him. The Doucet manuscript shows how he let his pen fly over the page, simply following the words as they emerged, submitting to the pressure exerted by the surge of his imagination, and to the speed that made it impossible to control the way the text unfolded. The proof of the authenticity of this writing style is demonstrated by the fact that, although the text is clearly inspired by *The Magnetic Fields*, it is no mere imitation. From its opening lines, *New Hebrides* sets itself apart from the striking imagery that characterises the first section of the earlier work, "The Unsilvered Glass" — "Prisoners of drops of water, we are but everlasting animals" — by adopting a deadpan narrative voice: "Aragon, Breton, Vitrac and I are living in an extraordinary house that backs on to the railway".

This narrative style sets the tone for the breathless way the rest of the episodes will unfold. The various adventures, catastrophes and coincidences that pile up and at the same time negate each other defy any notion of verisimilitude in the text. *New Hebrides* wants nothing to do with novelistic realism, seeking instead a specific kind of aesthetic accomplishment. Desnos delves as deeply as he can into his mental state to deliver a text that could be likened to a psychoanalytic cure. It is not a matter of going beyond language, but of going beyond literature. Although he is as much of a storyteller as Aragon, he doesn't intend, as Aragon does, to undermine literature from within, but rather, with all its risks and dangers, his aim is to renounce literature itself.

The influence of *The Poet Assassinated* (1916) is of a different order. For Apollinaire, storytelling offers not so much a means of exploring a new theory of writing, but the possibility of creating a narrative in which autobiographical elements are insinuated, in a veiled and allusive fashion, into the most unbridled fantastical imaginings. The burlesque myth of the poet is constructed through a series of wild and bawdy adventures in which the heroes take the form of puppet characters. The story's free expression and eccentricities are the fruit of a style of composition that leaves nothing to chance. *The Poet Assassinated* was put together by arranging various fragments written at different times, in the course of which the author's personal history is revealed through the fate of the poet Croniamantal. As Michel Décaudin has stated, "because of certain specific facts and the general outline of his life, including the failed novel, we know that Croniamantal is Apollinaire, and perhaps such an identification might even make it possible to discern the secret of Apollinaire's birth; but he is also the archetypal poet who, like Homer, kindles the legend and manages to elude the clutches of time."[7] When Desnos described how he was influenced by *The Poet Assassinated*, it is clear that he was attracted by the idea of exploring his innermost secrets in the most unfettered fictional forms. Apollinaire was of course aware of the originality of this type of storytelling: "It is an attempt at a new type of lyricism [...] that includes an element of satire."[8] *New Hebrides* owes a great deal of its hybrid nature to Apollinaire.

## *The Country of Demented Compasses and Clocks*

Desnos explained to Doucet the circumstances in which he began writing what would eventually become this book: "I wrote the first page one idle evening at the Petit Grillon café, in the Passage des Panoramas, while I was waiting for one of the main characters in the novel to turn up. I carried on after that wherever I was, in cafés (particularly a small bar on the Ile de la Cité which was popular with bargemen), on the train, in my room or at the office where I work." Desnos took to filling the time while he was left bored waiting for someone by concocting adventures in which the people who were keeping him waiting became characters in the service of his dreams. Instead of simply complying passively with a rather underwhelming reality, Desnos reacted by controlling it by means of his imagination.

"Aragon, Breton, Vitrac and I are living in an extraordinary house that backs on to the railway." With this introductory sentence, Desnos seems to set out the rules for this kind of writing: the reference to real, well-known people going hand in hand with the description of an imaginary location. Lived reality does not exclude the imaginary. It is the fixed point from which the momentum of the imaginary unfurls.

It is important here to distinguish between the various things being referred to. Whether they refer to people or places, the names in the text make their real impression even if none of this reality is upheld within the fantasy world of the narrative. The names are one kind of material amongst several others. And while the names Desnos introduces into his stories are certainly those of members of the *Littérature* group, the adventures they are plunged into obey no reality principles. The characters burst into the narrative bent on performing certain actions, or spouting sententious words, before vanishing again until the next time they appear. Benjamin Péret's arm, forever in pursuit of the narrator and trying, not without humour, to strangle him or to operate the guillotine's blade; Aragon galloping across the savanna alongside the narrator, then casting in bronze a monstrous statue "with a hundred and forty-three arms [and] seventy-nine legs" to replace the statue of Rimbaud; André Breton stopping time at ten past eight; the portraits of Vitrac, Baron, Monsieur and Madame Breton and Aragon nailed to the treads of the staircase, or Crevel's in the mirror at the Pelican Bar; Mr and Mrs Josephson and Malkine trying to maintain normal behaviour in a universe that has been turned upside down — as each of these examples shows, Desnos is obsessed by the thought of all his new friends. Other names also find their way into the narrative: Apollinaire, for example, who takes over half of the narrator's body, or Louis de Gonzague-Frick, a casualty of the flooding of Paris. In this way, a number of familiar names are written into the text in unexpected contexts, as the story irrepressibly unfolds.

Geographical pointers also play their role as token reminders of external reality. If many parts of the world are evoked at some point or other, it is Paris that is most haunted by the narrator's fantasies, and the only place where he experiences everyday reality. The Champs Elysées, the Champ de Mars, the Sacré-Cœur and the Eiffel Tower, the Place de la Concorde, the Place de l'Etoile, the banks of the Seine, the Gare Saint-Lazare, the aquarium at the Trocadéro and the Musée Grévin — the list could go on — are just a few of the places that provide the backdrop for car chases or are swallowed up by floods, places over which mysterious flying machines hover, at the mercy of images that are constantly metamorphosing within the dreamer's mind. "Demented compasses" are unable to locate north in this universe that is in constant flux. Miss Flowers finds a radium compass with two needles, one of which points to the South Pole and the other to an unknown direction — the direction the heroes will follow in the course of their adventure. This "inexplicable compass" will later be found nestled in Miss Flowers's navel.

The treatment of time is no less fantastical. References to actual moments in history or to the narrator's personal history can be made out, but they do not offer any fixed points or the least sense of continuity in the stories being told. "The short-circuiting clock" is a manifestation of this breakdown of temporality, as time itself contracts: *"The silences that separate the half-hours become shorter and shorter until they can no longer be distinguished from the very short silences that separate the knocks."* The clocks chime different hours in unison, pendulums lose control when their clocks strike twelve and the question "What time is it?" gets asked at repeated intervals as time no longer passes but stops definitively at ten past eight. In this malfunctioning time, nothing can be properly accomplished — living and dying are one and the same, and the dead are hale and hearty: "When I stood up, I discovered I was no longer alive," the narrator says at one point. Later on he kills Louis Morin and the

Captain, only for them to reappear in the next chapter.

These established references to identifiable people, places or dates, far from endorsing the reality of the text, instead contribute, paradoxically, to the "scant evidence of reality" found there, serving merely as a substratum to the dreamlike adventure. It is the same with all the more or less fleeting allusions to the narrator's personal experiences.

Perhaps the Ile de la Cité, where certain episodes of the narrative were written, was the inspiration for the other islands that emerge in the course of the tale, just as its little bar and the bargemen who frequented it inspired the character of the Captain and the brawls in the Pelican Bar. Desnos certainly seems to have found the names of some of the characters who pop up in the story in the articles he read while working as a secretary at the medical bookshop Baillères: "A man by the name of Diethyl-malonylurea and a woman called Hexamethylenetetramine wanted to protect the Eiffel Tower, which had sprung forth again from the generalised paralysis which is an early sign of Romberg syndrome, from which it suffers." Perhaps too some of the episodes in *New Hebrides* that contain themes revisited in Desnos's later works have their origins in the narrator's own experiences, for example, the near drowning of a young woman on 17 July 1916, the sensual daydreams stirred by parquet flooring, the orgasm brought on by being spanked by a woman's hand, or the thirteen-year-old boy's ambiguous erotic awakening during a holiday in England. The 1922 novel dramatises Desnos's personal erotic preferences — as vaunted in his 1923 essay, "On Eroticism" — and gives licence to the masochistic fantasies that would continue to haunt Desnos's later works.

## Maternal Desires and Miss Flowers

Whilst the stories presented in *New Hebrides* bear no relationship to any kind of realism, they are certainly filled with intense erotic obsessions. The ways in which this is dramatised may vary, but the fundamental themes remain constant. Thus, from the very first episodes there are repeated scenes of spanking. First there is the scene where the mother spanks her thirteen-year-old son in front of the whole family: "The mother lays her son across her legs, pulls down his pants, lifts up his shirt — and smacks his bottom! The three little cousins can barely contain their laughter, and his sister gasps in delight. The others look up from their eating and drinking. The mother is aroused by this sport; the boy comes in his mother's skirt." The action supposedly lasts for two hours, expanding to include all the characters, until "Everybody comes." Three new characters appear soon after — Louis Morin, the Captain and Miss Flowers — and the fantasy is played out once more on a little island just off the coast, where another boy, also thirteen, endures the "great noisy slaps" dealt him by the American woman. A similar scene is played out in Paris, where the victim is "a boy wearing make-up". Early childhood sensations are also evoked: "The Lyon *Courrier* has stolen my hymns in praise of parquet floors, across which I swim voluptuously towards unknown lands." This theme is made more general later on: "Boys' hearts leapt silently on to the crystal blades of the parquet, the shape of a woman appeared on each one". Earlier on, we also encounter "the mistress with hands so soft that you long to be chastised by them

[...] The English mistress who chastises you so tenderly." For it is "love's pains freely endured" that are at the heart of these stories.

As mistress of the game, the character of Miss Flowers stands out as she "gazes maternally" at the affectionate behaviour of the Captain and Louis Morin. She "poses like an American, rides horses and takes her breakfast in a beautiful pair of pyjamas", wields a riding-crop and likes switches.[9] Later she even takes on male sexual attributes in order to sodomise the homosexual thief who stole her jewels: "A flexible penis then grew out of the body of the young American woman". Once finished, "she sliced off the extra penis with her fingernails at the base, next to the testicles [...] She stood there, a woman once more."

What is Miss Flowers's relationship to the narrator? "Robert Desnos, you are in love with this woman. Why won't you tell her?" To this question, asked by an unnamed voice, he replies, "I feel ashamed." The narrator can probably be identified with the character of Louis Morin, Miss Flowers's homosexual victim, but he also remains distinct from the young man, imagining himself instead as the lover who fulfils her: "The young woman leaned over and kissed me on the lips", "I took the young American woman in my arms and feverishly we made love", "Miss Flowers never grew weary, and every morning she discovered a new burst of love and a caress for me". The young, lustful woman shows how skilled she is at all types of feminine seduction: "Naked from feet to waist, she wandered through the empty streets, a bodice of blue and silver-striped silk tucked tightly into her belt and domino gloves poking out from the ends of her sleeves. A string of pearls was clasped around her neck. A large hat with white feathers finished off the ensemble. Violinist, don't move, a little bird is about to emerge. The heart of her bottom and the triangle of her thighs. And sometimes her kisses in your ear." Their lovemaking takes on a cosmic dimension when Miss Flowers, having gulped down her partner's eyeballs, offers herself to him: "Her vagina, Africa, O Africa, where the equator bloomed, opened up like a gorgeous flower. I lay down inside to rest." In this dreamlike episode, where they become literally inseparable, Miss Flowers and the narrator represent the perfect couple, as is indicated by the phrase "Miss Flowers and I", repeated throughout.

In the course of these episodes, violent acts between the two transform into games of death. Miss Flowers herself becomes the victim of her lover: "I grabbed Miss Flowers by the hair [...] With great skill I cut off her right breast [...] I tore both thighs off the American woman [...] This woman I played with less than I did with red apple compote, or the song of a gosling in a ballroom."

### *Lessons from Childhood Reading*

On a narrative level, the episode in which the trapper is taken prisoner and tortured by Indians appears to have no connection to the narrator's adventures with Miss Flowers. In fact, according to a marginal note by Desnos (dated 1926) on the Corti manuscript, the story was inspired by a favourite children's book: "On 24 October 1926, I re-read *The Pirates of the Prairies*, by Gustave Aimard. I bought it for myself again three months ago, having not so much as glanced at it since 1912. Amazingly nostalgic, such precise memories (see page 272 onwards)."

Gustave Aimard is included on the list of those buried in the cemetery after the sinking of the *Sémillante*. Before writing his many serialised novels Aimard had experienced adventures himself while travelling through the American West; his books have the whiff of real life about them. *The Pirates of the Prairies* (1858) was one of the first he wrote after his return to France, and like all his books, has been republished several times. In various bloody battles, pirates (men who believe neither in God nor the law), hunters, trappers, Comanche and Apache Indians fight each other to the death using all manner of tricks and showing absolutely no mercy. Some of the adventures feature female characters — American women pitted against Spanish women — thereby spicing up the fights. Valentin Guillois, a French hunter known and respected throughout the prairies, features in all the battles. His name does not appear in *New Hebrides*, though Desnos took it as a pseudonym when he wrote the short story "Le Veilleur du Pont-au-Change" in 1944. An echo of Aimard's writing can be detected in *New Hebrides* in the extreme violence of the descriptions of torture, which comes to an end with a fire in which both the warring parties perish. In Aimard's original story the narrative continues with further episodes, but Desnos, exalting the heroism of the trapper when he is subjected to the most exquisite acts of cruelty, brings it to a two-fold climax. As Desnos conjures up complete devastation — "When the two fires, having joined together as one, died for want of fuel, there remained no trace of men or animals, alive or dead" — he then unexpectedly turns the narrative back to his erotic heroine: "That's how I met Miss Flowers." Is this a way of suggesting the inextricable link between Eros and Thanatos? Or is it simply a strategy to integrate the apparently autonomous Indian episode into the weft of the story?

As they accumulate, the narrative sequences seem quite naturally to take on the form of a serial that could apparently continue until the dreamer's imagination runs out of ideas. Amidst this whirlwind of adventures, a certain semblance of continuity is established — not through any logical sequence of events, but because of the repeated return of the various protagonists, and the obsessive focus on violence and extreme experiences. Structurally, the writing depends on the simple and artless repetition of unpolished description, alongside bombastic declarations and interludes in verse. All these elements considered, it could be argued that the writing is stymied by its lack of momentum. Has Desnos in fact been ensnared by repetition (as his dream world may suggest)?

From this perspective the episode with the trapper, in which Desnos explored the emotions aroused by reading Aimard when he was a child, perhaps can be seen as a desire for renewal. The use of automatic writing to explore his imaginary world clearly enabled him to travel to its furthest limits. The reader is hardly surprised at all when Desnos brings his experiment to an abrupt end, casting into the void all the characters he has brought to life in the sequence of stories. Alphonse Daudet's *Letters from my Windmill* provided the inspiration for the final pages of *New Hebrides*. In Daudet's book the sinking of the frigate *La Sémillante* is evoked by the cemetery that protects the memory of that terrible event: "How sad it was, the cemetery of *La Sémillante*! [...] I can see it still, with its little low wall, its rusty iron gate so hard to open, its silent chapel and the hundreds of black crosses hidden in the grass [...] Oh, those poor abandoned souls, how cold they must be, in their ill-starred tomb!"

The cemetery in *New Hebrides* is quite different from Daudet's: the individual graves are marked with names and neatly ordered around a common grave. Perhaps there is an ironic echo here of Valéry's "Graveyard by the Sea", published in 1920. With somewhat black humour Desnos buries his friends, both the famous and the less well known — and not forgetting to bury himself as well. Between the Doucet and the Corti manuscripts he made amendments to some of the names, but the tone remains the same. He must simply have decided it was time to end this experiment in automatic writing, for having only just established the burial plan, the story of his imaginary wanderings comes to a sudden end, as a sextant falls fatally on to the back of the narrator's head, "with a terrible noise that reproduced exactly this syllable: *PING*!"

It's a rather perfunctory way of bringing to an end the risky experiment in which Desnos, in search of himself, put his trust in words and their capacity to reveal hidden things. Both *Mourning for Mourning* and *Liberty or Love!* drew their erotic inspiration from *New Hebrides*, but their more conventional style allowed them to slip past the censors and find a publisher.

Marie-Claire Dumas

*Translator's Notes*

1. Jacques Doucet (1853-1929) was a fashion designer who built an important collection of manuscripts by contemporary writers, and also subsidised several of the Surrealists with a regular income in return for manuscripts etc. His archive was donated to the University of Paris in 1917, which established the Bibliothèque Littéraire Jacques Doucet after his death.
2. This was eventually published in 1953.
3. Alluded to by the narrator of the novel, who goes "to the Bibliothèque Nationale only to look at the obscene books".
4. In English in the original.
5. The *Sémillante* was carrying troops to the Crimea and sank in 1855 with the loss of 700 lives.
6. See Appendix I.
7. *Œuvres en Prose*, Pléiade, vol. I, p.1157.
8. *Ibid.*, pp.1158-9.
9. The word *"verge"* here inDesnos's text can signify either penis or a birch switch. The ambiguity is clearly intentional.

# THE PUNISHMENTS OF HELL, OR NEW HEBRIDES

Aragon, Breton, Vitrac and I are living in an extra ordinary house that backs on to the railway. Every morning I tiptoe down the stairs, the sound muffled by the three-coloured carpet, so as not to wake Madame Breton, who is still asleep. It's odd how the screeching locomotives howl on my time-bound wrist. Péret is waiting for me downstairs: we're off to a desert island. A Zanzibar is perhaps not for eating when there aren't any more little discs to put in the prismatic funnels. Péret falls asleep and I go out. As I walk past the fortifications the customs officers sneer at me and ask to see my driving licence. But I am on foot. Fawning smiles and coarse insults. I cut and run but they stay put in the doorway, waving their arms about and fussing with their hats. But there is no one to be seen in Paris, no one except an old shopkeeper who has died, her face submerged in a bowl overflowing with velvety smiles. The trams and buses are lined up in pairs. The midday streets are illuminated by electric lights. The clocks all chime different hours in unison.

I make my way home. On the stairs, portraits of Vitrac, Baron,

Monsieur and Madame Breton and Aragon are nailed to each tread. In Vitrac's bedroom there is a keg of whisky; in Aragon's a small trumpet, in Baron's a pile of old shoes, and on the door of Monsieur and Madame Breton's room a warning has been scrawled in chalk: *You're in for a serious hiding.* I go back, and Benjamin Péret's face is at the window. I run towards the desert island, which has been devastated by a volcanic eruption. Péret is standing on the small jetty waving at me, and has grown a huge beard, in which I get tangled as I wipe my feet.

Farewell Péret. Farewell! When Francis I died the orbs of his bright spheres left no trace on those windowpanes fastened with crepe. Farewell Péret.

The train passed by at great speed. Péret jumped on board, Benjamin *en route* for some chemical blooming. But he wasn't fast enough: one of his arms, the left one, remained suspended in the space above the platform. Five hundred kilometres down the line Benjamin was still gesticulating for me to send it on to him. Some flocks of sheep were trampling on the bell for the angelus and mats woven out of women's hair. To what end? I left Benjamin Péret's arm in the station marking time, Benjamin Péret's arm, alone in space, suspended over the platform, pointing towards the exit, and beyond, to the Grand Café du Progrès, and beyond… and beyond…

Tiny luminous filaments sprout from my woollens.

"Close the door to this compartment or I'll sound the alarm and all the horizontal towns one after the other.* The concierge whose wife gives birth once a minute is burning little ducks. He will not stop, and in fact, when he opens the door, we are going so fast that the pastel-coloured celluloid house is already far away, already in ruins, already destroyed, rebuilt and, who knows, perhaps inhabited by this man who stumbles as he capers about but does not manage to drag me away."

I shut my eyes. My magnificent mane — that irritates me and tickles me in certain places, as well as on my chin, the back of my neck and my ear — has a bit missing. Following myself I find that I am shrinking to the point where I can pass right through this gap, behind which I find myself on a mane with no obverse.

At night, on the Rue de Rivoli, women's voices emerging from a street-lamp: "Darling, would you gather me some bilious pigments from field number 3, in the countryside, just like in that little song?"

Field number 3? I made my way there walking on my hands. "And you know what, it was only a palace with thirty-six corridors planted with columns. A child was playing with the sun as its hoop and the number 3 divides the view into four parts."

A prophetess is making signs at me. The crowd cheers me on. The men have taken off their trousers and undergarments and are waving them above their heads. The wind frolics carelessly with their sexual parts. Some of these have even become aroused; the men in question are borne in triumph around a statue of a carafe and a telescope. The women, on the other hand, do not lift up their skirts. In my honour they scribble words in lipstick on the bellies of their husbands.

"Oh no, I don't want to be a one-armed man! Someone charter a train, a steamboat or a globe just for me and I'll leave, for I don't believe a person departs a station by the door or the windows, but by ladders that climb eternally towards the horizon."

The whole family is sitting around the festive table: father, mother, the son (aged thirteen), the daughter (fifteen) and three cousins (eleven, twelve and thirteen). An uncle and an aunt. When they get to dessert, father recites a traditional speech in verse:

> *My beard which on itself does curl*
> *has made processions to unfurl*
> *like that of Saint André du Roule*
> *and mirror how it moves in full.*
>
> *Take heed my children, learn from these,*
> *this moral of the bunch of keys,*
> *that was bestowed on you at birth*
> *by a broom-borne mistress dropped to earth*

The three cousins and the daughter then play a piece on bottle bottoms for eight hands. The boy recounts a fable:

> *The basis clear of my justice*
> *is unknown to the best athlete.*
> *The moral: ferments of hot piss*
> *are in the child that's yet at teat.*

The mother lays her son across her legs, pulls down his pants, lifts up his shirt — and smacks his bottom! The three little cousins can barely contain their laughter, and his sister gasps in delight. The others look up from their eating and drinking. The mother is aroused by this sport; the boy comes in his mother's skirt. Two hours later she finally stops, but that red bottom is so beautiful now that none of them can stop looking at it. He kneels in a corner, with his shirt pulled up to his shoulders and his pants down.

An hour later, in the bedroom next door, his sister (aged fifteen) and her eldest cousin are spanking the other two little girls. Everybody comes. The other characters have shut themselves away.

Ten years later the four girls have become whores at the Taverne de l'Olympia;* their parents are disabled lace-makers and the son is a ship's captain on the high seas. It was he who brought me back my hat after the wind had carried it all the way to the New Hebrides.

Since then I have started work again on my book on mathematics.

I go to the Bibliothèque Nationale only to look at the obscene books and I am willing to make love to absolutely anybody.

My nostrils are the entrance to an echoing subway. My friend Baignoire,* my girlfriend, my girlfriend Verdure,* my friend — where are we going?

This bottle of rum puts me irresistibly in mind of the Magdeburg hemispheres,* and if, sometimes, memories of the war lead me all the way to the sun, other thoughts still penetrate my brain with their parallel banners. That's the story of my life.

Small soldiers in red knickerbockers in a horse-drawn carriage in the rain, and the sinister song of this subway is the axis of my heart. I am the path through the virgin forests which mark the edge of the pavements. It would be a crime to tread on these shadows, so silent and filled with evil intentions. The Lyon *Courrier* has stolen my hymns in praise of parquet floors, across which I swim voluptuously towards unknown lands. At the supreme moment, as I find myself drowning, I half close my eyes and the features of my face slip down towards my navel until I look like that fat old gentleman with a lantern instead of a name.

The mistress with hands so soft that you long to be chastised by them. Why do they piss and spit so far? I don't have the strength for that. Twelve flags run up for my England at dawn. The English mistress who chastises you so tenderly. The cricket I swallow will keep on singing for as long as it lives.

This is the song of the watercress-seller:

> *I'll never have a horrid spider to restore*
> *These tiny holes with dashes here of flowery lace.*
> *My God! My God! Bring back the noisy tricolor,*
> *Return the love of honour to this tidal space.*

Now that I am as old as a young captain, now that the staircase opens up before me, after the door has closed, up I go. A light-bulb on each landing, the silence, and I am afraid of who is not there. My blood rises after me all the way up to my lower lip. Quickly, quickly, up I go, quickly, and all night long I keep on falling down.

My shadow is up on the roof of the hangar, tangled up with something or someone else's shadow. What a disappointment not to be able to project the one thing that belongs to me alone. I hold my arm out. The wind casts it back. I am only truly alone in a crowd.

Love's pains freely endured and bonbons dressed in sailor suits were my chaperones on this adventure.

*The stage is illuminated by a light-bulb. A policeman, standing motionless. A long silence. The clock strikes three. Silence. A knock. Enter Baignoire and Verdure.*

BAIGNOIRE: The wire ribbon loves the sprung silence of the incredible parachute.

VERDURE: My dream was of waxen sleep, but I was borne away on small swaying telephonic clouds, stuffed with ingenious designs.

BAIGNOIRE: Rich perfume and tokens of victory, the sound of tear-gas in the sleeves of permanent fiancées.

VERDURE: Error. The heart of this silence has been softened by the leak in the dark pipes where academicians hold out their caduceus caps and beg for alms from the red umbrellas.

BAIGNOIRE: Here's your Métro ticket.

VERDURE: My ticket, yours and your suitcase.

BAIGNOIRE: Your suitcase, mine and your blanket.

VERDURE: My blanket, yours and our two tickets.

BAIGNOIRE: What is the point of caging wild animals behind such a flimsy barrier? Those strange geophagi who get the horizon rolling repeat the same callous words to persuade them to remain sedentary.

## THE SHORT-CIRCUITING CLOCK

*On the three sides of the stage are coloured check curtains. There is no sign of a door or a window. Entrances and exits are accomplished by raising the curtains. A table and two chairs.*

### DRAMATIS PERSONAE

THE BULB, very big, hangs very low on a cord above the table. It is on. It is the only illumination on the stage.

THE TIMEPIECE: On the table stands an alarm-clock, preferably with a loud ring.

THE POLICEMAN: Made of bran and fabric. Leaning against the wall in a corner.

BAIGNOIRE/VERDURE: Age, sex and costume *ad libitum.*

VERDURE: Go back upstairs and show her the handsome pole.

BAIGNOIRE: One cannot be and have been.

[*They leave. Long silence.*]

THE POLICEMAN: Why didn't they turn the electricity off?

*A long silence, then the clock strikes four. Silence. A knock. Silence. Five knocks. Silence… And so on. Once the knocking reaches twelve it starts again. The silences that separate the half-hours become shorter and shorter until they can no longer be distinguished from the very short silences that separate the knocks. The policeman made from bran and fabric falls to the ground. The clock strikes continuously. The curtain falls.*

"Robert Desnos, you are in love with this woman. Why won't you tell her?"

"I feel ashamed."

"Robert Desnos, it is not shame that stops you from speaking, and what is more, you are not sentimental."

"It is true that I am not sentimental, but I am a creature capable of affection. It is fun playing roulette with the wheel spinning on your podex."

"Robert Desnos, you love your friends."

"I know this woman. She is the mother of a fourteen-year-old girl. With her sensuous lips this girl is skilled at preparing her lovers for the delights her mother offers. Don't talk to me about Baignoire. He spies on his son's homosexual acts from the other side of the wall, mimicking with his right hand the swinging of the pendulum. You know, the kind of pendulum that loses control at the twelfth hour."

At the beach, Louis Morin is waiting to go for a swim. He is thirteen years old, and staying in a guesthouse. The Captain and Miss Flowers arrive. The Captain is young, handsome and quite uncomplicated; Miss Flowers poses like an American, rides horses and takes her breakfast in a beautiful pair of pyjamas. The three of them are going to go swimming. A hundred metres from the beach there is a tiny island. They swim towards it, and when they get there they wade up on to the sand. On the side of the island facing the mainland there is a beach, and the three of them lie down. While he is lying there on his stomach, Miss Flowers suddenly squats down on Louis Morin's shoulders. He hammers his feet on the sand, quite taken by surprise. Miss Flowers is heavy, and her body smells good through her swimming costume. Louis Morin is young, aroused but exhausted. Five minutes later the handsome Captain, stretched out on the sand, lets out a sigh and screws up his eyes. Miss Flowers is comforting Louis, who, stripped of his underpants, is quietly moaning and whimpering. In America, boys his age are frequently beaten. Miss Flowers is hot, and takes her mind off it by giving him great noisy slaps. Louis Morin doesn't even have the strength to cry out any more, his bottom just twitches and tenses as it moves up and down. When they swim back to the mainland he has to cling on to the Captain and Miss Flowers. When they are out for a stroll that evening he offers his arm to the officer. The American woman, gazing at them maternally, offers them sweets and tells them stories. When her hand brushes against the boy he blushes and lowers his eyes.

During the days that follow the three of them never leave one another's side. They swim twice a day; Louis Morin is having trouble walking. The American woman goes to Paris. A boy wearing make-up is wandering around the Gare Saint-Lazare. The two of them go to a hotel. What could she possibly want of me?

"Would you let me do it?"

She takes off his jacket, waistcoat, shirt, trousers and underpants. He is naked. He is still wearing his black shoes and his grey stockings are attached by suspenders to a black belt which holds his stomach in and makes his bottom stick out.

"How handsome he is."

"Do you think so?"

"Come here."

He still won't have got over this by the next morning.

The Captain, meanwhile, goes upstairs.

"What does Monsieur desire? A little boy? A little girl?"

"I would like an armchair and the *Daily Mail.*"

Louis Morin arrives.

"Good morning, young man, how are you? What can I do for you?"

"A single bed."

Miss Flowers arrives.

"What can I do for you?"

"My horse and riding-crop and three girls in black stockings, with black shoes and red garters... each with two switches."

"Two switches?"

"Exactly, and make sure they're good-quality birch."

"Good morning Captain, good morning, little Louis."

"Good morning Miss, good morning."

"So, here's the story," says the pretty girl. "I stopped off at the Pelican Bar, with a pearl necklace in each hand and my diamonds wrapped around my ankles. The negro saxophonist stopped playing. He was dead. Another musician quickly replaced him. The conductor was sitting down; he was dead. A boy took his place. The pianist cried out; he was still-born. Someone closed the lid of the piano. I turned and saw the homosexual running off down the street with my diamonds and my two pearl necklaces. So I came to find you."

"And a good thing you did," said the Captain, and with one movement he smashed three windowpanes and the light-bulb too. The three of them went out into the street.

I happened to be walking by just at that moment. Benjamin Péret had returned to his compartment in the train and Paris was empty. On the Boulevard Montparnasse, the Captain stopped, put his finger to his lips: *shhh!* and dived into the shadows of a *porte cochère.**

On the Place de la Concorde Louis Morin stopped, and threw his hat to the ground. "How careless," he cried, "how careless, he will never get over it!" He wept and clung on to our arms.

"What is he talking about?" asked Miss Flowers.

I didn't know.

"You wouldn't understand," replied the boy, "but wait here for me. If I haven't returned in one hour, it will be up to you to avenge us."

And he disappeared in the direction of the Boulevard Saint-Germain.

Miss Flowers and I found ourselves standing alone in the gloomy shadows of the unlit Place de la Concorde. Because the city had been deserted the gas had been burning for eleven days straight and the electricity had stayed on for a week, but since the previous evening it had all gone out, even the little red lamps that indicate a construction site or a street that has been closed off.

A short while after Morin had left, three clocks sounded: the first struck twice, the second struck seven and the third struck eleven times. Miss Flowers kissed me on the mouth.

"Is it true," I asked, "is it true that acidic waters are eating into the piles of the bridges and that the big red and blue question-marks standing beside the high-speed railways have been extinguished for ever?"

I knew several cities and the names of many women. But this tongue and these lips had a smell and a taste known only to the admirers of Senegalese goddesses or those who come from the place where I was born.

Miss Flowers laid her hand on my arm. And just then, somewhere in the distance, there came a gunshot, then another, then a third. Someone close by sighed deeply, but the night was so dark we couldn't make out a thing. Behind Notre Dame and the Palais Bourbon, violently coloured flares rose up slowly into the sky, never to come back down. The three clocks chimed. In spite of the distance we could distinctly hear the mechanical clicks and the movement of their toothed wheels as they engaged. Then from some way off, the unmistakable crack of three more gunshots.

"Let's go," said Miss Flowers. "They are dead, for certain they are dead."

We stepped out on to the Champs Elysées. We could hear the sound of a funfair through the trees but couldn't make out where it was coming from.

Every now and then, from somewhere in the deserted city, we heard the long, drawn-out cry — and yet it seemed so close — of the locomotives. What locomotives? The Place de l'Etoile was gloomy and deserted.

Miss Flowers stopped.

"Love that is multiplied," she said, "knows the secret of mouths turned inside out. Seashells lie scattered along the path of alkaloid lovers. The Numidian warrior who possessed me knew how to maintain his dignified self-control during our whispered congress. Listen not to your muscles as they speak, nor to the chant of vertical columns of smoke in your mechanical ears."

The floodlight crushed the historical figures on the wet tarmac into which the street-lamps were sinking as one by one I lit them with wax matches. Once the whole square was lit up my companion dragged me into a corner and said:

"The diamonds and the two pearl necklaces stolen by the homosexual grant whoever holds them in their possession access to the most powerful throne on Earth. I know that the monarch is almost at his last gasp. We must find the necklaces and the diamonds, Robert Desnos, we must."

"Yes," I replied, "and we must also avenge our companions."

Day was breaking, Paris was still enveloped in its own silence, and the cobblestones, washed clean by the recent rain, ran endlessly into the distance. Under the pale sky two disused tracks continued towards the unknown. The other two didn't even do that.

"See you tonight," said Flowers. "Go and get some sleep. We'll meet this evening at the Pelican Bar, there'll be nobody there."

I went back to my marvellous house beside the railway. It was still deserted. The photographs nailed to the blue white red treads of the staircase were beginning to yellow.

First I sat down in an armchair and then I went to bed.

Benjamin Péret appeared at the window.

"The homosexual gem thief has hidden the jewels under the arches of two metal bridges. You must find them tonight if you want to win over the beautiful American woman you're in love with. Evil powers are watching you, intent on your downfall. There's no point consulting the cards, you should sleep. Tomorrow night this whole struggle will get violent. As soon as you wake up, get your car ready, and be sure to load your revolvers beforehand."

I awoke at five o'clock that afternoon. I filled the racing car's tank, placed six revolvers within easy reach, switched on the right headlight and set off for the Pelican Bar. The musicians were on stage, rotting; Miss Flowers hadn't turned up. I mixed a few cocktails and put them in pairs on various tables. I watched as they were drained by invisible mouths. I knew what I wanted. In one leap I was outside. I slammed the door and kicked the bolts into place then sped off in my car after the kidnappers. I could hear Miss Flowers as she cried out for me to save her. I gave no reply, so as not to alert them to my presence. I noticed that each time the bandits' car came to a bend in the road, one of them sounded a fireman's siren as the car took the corner. And the undetected pursuit of the pursued crossed Paris under the gaze of those demented pneumatic clocks.

I caught up with the car in front, and got a glimpse of Flowers, naked from her feet to her waist. She was wearing a black and red-striped bodice, a gold necklace and a felt hat. At the wheel was the Captain and next to him was Louis Morin.

They still hadn't seen me, so I fired off two shots from one of the revolvers. The car stopped. The Captain and Louis Morin were dead. Miss Flowers climbed into the passenger seat beside me and our car took off again in the direction of the Seine. My gaze fell to the black triangle outlined between the clenched, naked thighs of my companion.

"The angels' salvation," I said, "has breathed in the vegetable scent of the funeral wreaths of new cars on rainy days. Did you notice the guard was weeping at the corner where the steel gate is? Hand me the jewel please, the lovely electric jewel…" But my words stopped there. The young woman leaned over and kissed me on the lips. When I looked up again we were at the Passy Bridge. Miss Flowers got out. Five minutes later she reappeared with the necklaces and the diamonds. She fashioned them into a belt and we drove off. A little later the dawn rose like a curtain. In the windows of Paris green flags had blossomed, embroidered with red triangles and the word *Whisky*.

The air was still. All was quiet. We left the city by Porte Maillot.

We drove on by main roads and narrow lanes until we reached Bordeaux. There, waiting for us, was a boat that was about to depart. As soon as we were on board it set sail, and a few hours later we disembarked at Casablanca, where we were welcomed by a giant crane that was laying the foundations of the jetty.

At the head of the jetty an arid landscape dotted with dwarf palms stretched out ahead of us. As we approached, a camel got to its feet and trotted away. We walked for a hundred metres and ended up by an electric street-lamp and a stone pavement some ten metres long. There was no other sign of habitation.

"This is Casablanca," my companion said. She twisted the pearls around her hips and groin and the diamonds round her ankles, then exclaimed:

"The king has died of fright at the hollows in Italic songs; I am queen."

Night fell suddenly and the street-lamp came on.

I took the young American woman in my arms and feverishly we made love as the mist bellowed in the harbour. After two hours of passion we got to our feet and, leaving the street-lamp to illuminate the surrounding desert, we returned to the boat.

Off the coast of Spain the ship's captain came up to speak to me.

"Don't you recognise me? I once brought you back a hat that had been carried away by the wind to the New Hebrides, and my sister and cousins drank cocktails with you at the Taverne de l'Olympia." With a flourish, he ripped off his beard.

"The Captain!" I cried. "But I killed you and Louis Morin a few days ago back in Paris, as I was freeing my mistress."

The Captain laughed. Then he took me by the hand and led me to the prow of the boat. There, naked and covered in blue tattoos, was Louis Morin — impaled. The wind was spinning him in all directions, and every so often he gave a deep sigh.

"You see," said the Captain, "he isn't dead." He called over three sailors who took the child down from the stake. Blood trickled down his thighs and calves. They wiped him down with a sponge and the three of us went to Miss Flowers's cabin.

Watched by the Captain and his companion, she lit a cigarette and offered one to each of us. We finished the evening drinking port and cherry brandy and eating octopus mayonnaise, which tasted remarkably like lobster.

Night fell with the sound of breaking glass. We each went to our own cabins and I fell asleep almost immediately. I was awakened not long after by a faint thud at the porthole. An arm was reaching through it. From the button on the cuff I could see that it was Benjamin Péret's arm, the one I had left behind at the station. It made its way towards me and its hand grabbed me by the neck, it would have strangled me if I hadn't uttered the fateful word "Araucaria". At once the grip loosened, and the arm opened the door and disappeared down the corridor. I fell asleep again. The next morning Miss Flowers appeared wearing riding breeches and boots.

"Did the arm beat you up as well?" she asked me.

"No, but it did try to strangle me." The Captain and Louis Morin let out squawks of laughter.

Not long after we made land.

Paris was mechanically murmuring songs to the regular sobbing of the metallic bridges. Footsteps had worn furrows into all the streets. We made our way to the scene of the crime. Benjamin Péret's arm was still clutching at the necks of various corpses. With loud exclamations, it moved off. As for the corpses, they stood up and disappeared around the corner.

At the Pelican Bar, wild ducks were playing international hopscotch. On the door was written the following:*

$$x = \frac{-b \pm \sqrt{b^2 - 4ac}}{2a}$$

Without stopping to read we opened the door and settled down to drink port until the day was done. The next morning, as we were walking down the Champs Elysées, we saw a carousel with wooden horses at the Rond Point. We went towards it. Even though there was no one on it, it kept on turning, rhythmically and mathematically.

There were ears and mouths wandering about in the atmosphere. Some of the lips parted slightly so as to stick out their tongues at us, and that was all. The next day, for no reason, eyeballs were found stuck to all the keyholes and windowpanes, and we had to burst them with needles so we could get back into our apartment. Miss Flowers had once again abandoned her nether garments. Naked from feet to waist, she wandered through the empty streets, a bodice of blue and silver-striped silk tucked tightly into her belt and domino gloves poking out from the ends of her sleeves. A string of pearls was clasped around her neck. A large hat with white feathers finished off the ensemble. Violinist, don't move, a little bird is about to emerge. The heart of her bottom and the triangle of her thighs. And sometimes her kisses in your ear. On the fifth day the Eiffel Tower plunged noiselessly into the ground. In its place a fountain of saltwater fish gushed forth, from which crabs made their escape along the avenues and boulevards. On the sixth day my mistress showed me inside the buildings where the elevators kept going tirelessly up and down. On the seventh day the fire alarms lit up brighter than the sun the crossroads where pharmacies were clustered, and from here came the howling of locomotives and the shrieking of horns.

I was tired of living in the signal house. Besides, there was no let up from the taps as they poured sheet music and churches down the stairs. One day I ventured into a brothel. An enormous phallus lived there all on its own. It was pierced right through with a pin. Toothbrushes served as rugs and the phallus said to me:

"If you blush at an old codger of an accordion, what will the bells say?"

"If the bells turn the blue tint of the sunflower yellow, what will the phonographs say?"

"If inside their horns the blue turns into a bird, what will your mother say to that, what will your father say then?"

"Oh, don't bother trying to do anything apart from wearing out the pavement and the road by rubbing your hands on them. Two-way mirrors simulate impossible shipwrecks, while the greasy poles must not transform the useless momentum of arrows and mortar shells into a pointless vertical effort. Compasses disguised as navels will jeer at the caretakers of public squares. Street-lamps will tie themselves together at their middles and this is the prophecy of the male sex free of pox, free of desire free of rejection free of disgust."

I left without replying. The electric light-bulbs were being drained by syringes, which meant that the congress of the Suns threatened, if it continued, to discharge small creatures and oil drums all over the pavements. The syringes took no notice at all and the rivulets poisoned the fish in a sign of mourning.

A man by the name of Diethylmalonylurea and a woman called Hexamethylenetetramine wanted to protect the Eiffel Tower, which had sprung forth again from the generalised paralysis which is an early sign of Romberg syndrome, from which it suffers. Their efforts led to them contracting embarrassing diseases, and they were chased out of the city in shame.

One balmy evening the moths reappeared. All night long they fluttered around our cigarettes; at daybreak they flew off, leaving a pile of ashes at our feet and that was all.

Miss Flowers never grew weary, and every morning she discovered a new burst of love and a caress for me. Nor was I ever weary; and that is how we loved each other in that orthopaedic town.

The Captain had cloistered himself away I know not where with Louis Morin. Sometimes the sound of their voices reached us by telephone. But we dared not pick up the receiver because every time we did we heard this:

"Hello. Hello.

"The whiteness of pills, passion at five in the afternoon. The Zebu Boot Café, Africa, and the flag with the opera fumes that sad to the Eleanor in flowers have made their point with the switchblades of the green and white enamel knives. The Monsieur Poincaré star gives a decisive speech in Nancy. Russian children have been devoured by their American rescuers. The dollar at 2.50 francs a metre the stock exchange of injections with hour dials of radium and the carelessness of public services for the anaemias of the financial nemesis inspected on the Rhine. Cute little thing. Stop. Hello. Hello. The lawyer who stamps on a perfume has broken the heart of papa's marriage. Milk — Cocoa — Dubonnet."

Some nights, spindly human beings would come out of this machine and cut the cords of the double curtains.

That's why we don't use the telephone any more.

To the bobbing of four life buoys we siphoned off the doves that had been dispersed all over Paris. Our memories transformed the tarmac into alphabetic filaments that wrote our names in corridors of hydrophilic cotton. Standing on the hollow oxygen pedestal, the Captain spoke:

"I know the secret of the acoustic tube the caravans plug into for domestic discord. A penholder, at exactly noon, a pepper-pot at the far end of a promontory, a revolver lucky in love — all of these make a greater impression on my memory than Miss Flowers's tongue by the light of my small nocturnal sconces.

"The forest where I strung up my vices is greasy with a sweet-smelling oil. A concert of choke pears blows fright between two roaring mineral eyes.

"A clan of Merovingians rising up from the deepest of sympathetic regions tells all comers the formula for acid and about the silence of swans."

Then Louis Morin appeared. With a single thrust, he plunged a dagger into the Captain's dynamo lungs. The Captain, without saying a word, held out his cane and his glove to the adolescent. Two nurses led him to a nearby lake, and from there we could hear him giving orders to the army of tempestuous waves.

"My bedroom is sealed off on the alluvial plain," said Louis Morin. "A flower-bed of trombones is tallying up the odds for the jockeys who are beyond description. The Leonid stars raise the eardrums of the barbarian ladybirds." And then he sang a song:

> *In moonlight on the towpath free*
> *There skulked a man with candles three*
> *The maid who goads him on to more*
> *Has wrecked the Pont des Arts entire*
> *Give me a dose of bollocks sore*
> *And have I crackers still to fire?*

"Nothing else will do to straighten out my rutting. Disembowelled cruise ships flood the grassed-over reservoirs with rum and set it alight, and on top of the tomb of a respectable old man I made love to an eighteen-year-old girl. Kneeling in prayer, she could guide me right inside her because she was naked. And ever since then, bleeding and in pain, she waits with her thighs all awash with blood for the rutting of passers-by, each hoping they'll be the one who will at last stave in her matrimonial tympanum."

Resplendent and terrifying, Miss Flowers held her hand over the cowering form of the cynical homosexual. Soon, his clothes would be no more than rags in the stream. A flexible penis then grew out of the body of the young American woman, and she set about repeating the sodomised virgin's ordeal. Once the boy was bent over and held fast in this humiliating position she sliced off the extra penis with her fingernails at the base, next to the testicles, leaving it to its spasms inside his shaking body. She stood there, a woman once more, splendid in her two acetylene breast-shields, while her victim spewed out lakes of light and adulterated alcohol.

Seventeen years later I passed by that place again. Louis Morin, whimpering and seemingly no older, was still there in the same position.

Miss Flowers and I departed. In a hospital, eighteen flat-stomached girls had been connected to bicycle pumps. These balloons would burst when they reached the tropics. Eaten up by cancer, eighteen times the suffering mother prostituted herself in the astrological kennels, and a smear of mayonnaise became the emblem for this part of our adventure.

Baignoire and Verdure, transformed into a staircase, led us to the top of a skyscraper. On each floor, naked women were throwing themselves out of the windows. A phallic cup-and-ball lit up the uninhabitable city and the old people fleeing from it.

Arriving at the thirty-seventh floor, we saw that we were alone. The staircase vanished. At our feet the phallus was waiting for us, running its wet tongue over its lips. With one cry we threw ourselves into space.

Sailing-boats gave us shelter in the north of Ireland, bits of coral fell endlessly from the sky and the waves covered us with writing. This is what was written on the body of Miss Flowers:

> *Three women still alive impaled*
> *like artificial flowers they seem*
> *Upon its banks the Seine exhaled*
> *the virgins' relics from the stream*
>
> *Your lovers' neither here nor there*
> *were severed by your lips for good*
> *it is the stake that will lay bare*
> *your bush, that's clearly understood.*

Do not reckon up the catalogue from back to front. Criminals pour their heart and soul into the three doors of the music hall. Scheming and quarrelsome, this is the loveliest of all the squirrel foetuses and in the name of the God of my fathers: coach and horses.

A single word was written across my belly: *Cornwall.*

Straight away I felt enormous pride at this. I bruised the rails with my reckless leaps and all of a sudden the Place de la Concorde was filled with small basset hounds howling for the moon that wasn't there.

Withering in its silence, my hope appeared just then in a woman's pleated skirt, but Miss Flowers, disguised as a man, was chasing Cesare Borgia's *fishy poisons* in a street-lamp aquarium.

"I wouldn't know how to work out how to read this timetable," declared the body parts squirming about on the pavement. I recognised the heads of Baignoire and Verdure. The two of them had been chopped up into pieces and the matching parts of their bodies spoke together in chorus:

Mouths:  We bite the summits snowy with the flanks of heifers
     the colour of a bastard dandy.

Feet:   Thin scalp thin skin here
     Is the ideal of numerical prawns.
     Abandon your teeth
     Abandon your intestines
     Abandon the pupils of your eyes that have no music
     And Niagara will explode into African colonels
     devoured by Burgraves.*

Intestines: The door-latch and the grieving of steamers and music
     boxes have not brought Christ back from the dead. We
     have crept long enough in search of the boa
     constrictor
     that turns out to be no more than a magnificent
     burst of laughter in the purgatory of our inoculated
     ears.

Horrified, I fled up the Rue Royale. The squirming limbs went ahead of me and, surrounded by this company, I found myself all of a sudden standing in front of the door to my house. Shutting myself inside was child's play.

A steam-powered film projector showed me the incredible lusts to which Benjamin Péret had lent his voice and his puritanical criticism.

Shut up in my bedroom I could hear him fighting off multitudes of lizards whose eyes pierced the walls with X-rays. Eventually, unable to stand it any longer, I opened the door. The corpse of our poor friend was skulking in the shadows. Then he vanished.

Without a mistress, without a friend, without a conflict, I fell asleep. When I awoke, very thin but very strong lines had been attached to the dead suns on the ceiling of my room. As I got up they began to whir and spin in giddy circles. All the while, my room was changing shape, its elastic walls warping first into an ovoid, then a circle, then all at once a large triangle in which Egyptian queens were martyring my collection of rare animals. Undaunted by this, I looked at my reflection in the mirror, where, in amongst the seaweed and the seals, spectres wreathed in black pressed around a small wheel which too was whirring and spinning dizzily. The straight road was trundling along on invisible wheels. Children's heads made a muffled sound as they rolled through the sewers. A pretty breast stopped me at the junction of two boulevards. A flower was growing where the pink nipple should have been, and from which I would have liked to suck the Minervan calomel.

The flower was soon fully grown and its five petals scrolled through five ever-changing colours. Little by little the petals began turning and whirring giddily.

Finally the whole thing exploded. I found myself half-buried beneath the remains of the three Egyptian queens who had been loitering in my pyramid.

When I stood up, I discovered I was no longer alive. A silent aquatic world was pummelling the insides of my temples while insatiable pikes looked out through the windows of my eyes as Miss Flowers, located at last, approached me.

"Friend," she said to me, "a strange octopus is clutching the sponge from which the blood in my fingers seeks its substance. I am dead and so must you be too, since we can both see and hear each other." A kiss bound our lips and in the embrace our tongues changed places, and since then each of us has been condemned only to utter the thoughts of the other.

A short time afterwards I was admitted into the throne-room.

Miss Flowers stood up, and just as I was about to kneel and kiss her naked thighs she said, "A maidenhood has flowered once again within me. It is made of chrome steel and of those who strive for Catholic sainthood. All the rams in the world could not tear it asunder. If once I was the one you desired, she whose deep and inner places your member could not touch, henceforth I am the queen of posterior and material love."

She walked past me and was gone before I could utter a single word.

I could see now that up from the seat of the throne there rose a penis made of ivory and coral. As big as she wanted it to be, it adapted itself precisely to the anatomy of my mistress whose reign was thus one of perpetual pleasure. Many a Queen, held motionless on this virile seat, had looked upon their undeflowered sexual parts. Many a King, in the splendour of his youth, had there ridden his solitary proud pivot. Later on they let their beards grow to hide from the crowds their useless genitalia, withered from inactivity.

But as for this member made of inert materials, all I wanted to know was what relations it had had with the woman I would never again possess.

I lowered my lips towards its coral glans. Hardly had my kiss brushed against it than invisible clarinets began playing the same note over and over again. There was a puff of smoke, and in place of the phallus I saw Vitrac. He was carrying his head under his arm, and then with a single movement he put it between his legs. I noticed that he was wearing neither bathing trunks nor any underwear. On the front of his shirt were the words:

HONOUR, FATHERLAND

and on the back:

MARENGO PAUL DEROULEDE SALMON

As for his head, it was spinning round in all directions even as it licked him. At the crowning moment Vitrac opened his mouth. A swarm of phalluses flew out and began lining up on either side of the road.

A voice announced: "Monsieur André Breton." Immediately the phalluses turned into street-lamps with reflectors so that all at once I saw twenty-five likenesses of Monsieur André Breton coming in. He held out his hands to me and repeated twenty-five times:

> *Mikado in his shop was pressed*
> *to fade the flowering dove he kept*
> *The empress sliced off both her breasts*
> *her comb bit once, and then she wept*

He walked past me. The phalluses resumed their original form. A voice announced: "Madame Breton." The road was now only bordered with small columns like a picket fence. Philippe Soupault was standing on one leg on top of each of the columns. In his right hand he held a rose-bush. He sang:

> *The arse the sea the artichoke*
> *have rattled hard three promontories*
> *Now one old prof of history*
> *this recent mystery will evoke*
>
> *A schoolboy setting off to travel*
> *his new umbrella takes along*
> *the husband of a wife who wrongs*
> *then sticks it in her hollow navel.*

Just then Madame Breton appeared. I watched as she approached in silence. Every ten metres she went and stood in the stream. When she stepped out again her image remained behind. At this, the concierge of a nearby building was filled with a sense of great resentment. He called his son to him and the two of them ran off after Madame Breton. Panicked, and completely forgetting that I was dead, I rushed to her aid, but all the images in the stream had surrounded the two wretches. When I got there I saw that they had been chopped into tiny pieces. Madame Breton looked at me. She held out her hand and said:

*The flower of the stream is pretending to be a dirigible.*
*How I regret your death.*
*A ghastly adventure*
*will modify this unhappy fate*
*you need only consider*
*that the hypotenuse and planets*
*are beacons at liberty*
*that will give you back your lovely silhouette.*


She disappeared.

The phalluses reappeared. On each one the concierge and his son were impaled, in alternating sequence.

In the middle of the road, sitting on a chair, Philippe Soupault was playing the guitar. Passing motorists threw flowers and confetti at him, and there was soon a large pile beside him. Brusquely he swept it all away and the sky was filled with pretty aeroplanes. Soupault was keeping hold of them by a number of silken threads gathered up in one hand and thus accompanied he left the cemetery where my shade was finally dissolving into white circles in a cup of coffee.

Max Morise lifted the cup to his lips. Scarcely had he done so when green hairs began to sprout all over his body. They were bursting through the sleeves of his jacket and the legs of his breeches, and I found this so funny that when he tried to slip away dragging this fleece behind him, my laughter uprooted a vacant calvary right out of the ground.

The Pope was determined to see the work of the Devil in this. He came by car and in person to sprinkle quinquina* over it from a small crystal funnel. Thanks to this I was able to bring the dead back to life and allocate them to neighbouring stars and send the Pope to the bottom of the Seine from where he would never be able to escape.

I was extremely embarrassed to find myself stark naked in the middle of the cemetery. The dead that had been scattered amongst the stars flung crude abuse at me. I was thinking of returning to my grave when I felt a hand on my shoulder. I turned round and there was Louis Aragon. He was wearing wide cowboy breeches and an open-necked black silk shirt. A big sombrero hung from his belt on the right, on his head he wore a diamond crown and on his right arm was the armband from his first communion. He handed it to me swiftly so that I could use it to cover my genitals. We left.

In the street, the girls kept sneaking looks at us. Each was blind in her right eye and they sang in chorus:

> *The polyglot with legs off course*
> *taught us the code of Samuel Morse*

*to go to the pole of the old whale-horse\**
*to learn love's secret and its force.*

Passing in front of a mirror, I saw that the armband was twitching against my belly. I moved my hand there, and caught hold of a long bi-coloured snake which whispered in my ear:

*As winter shakes at bamboo's tip*
*and cylinders from Hell are thrown*
*She holds the right end in her grip*
*her little soldier can but moan.*

But I wasn't really listening. I made the snake into a lasso and swung it with all my might in the direction of a herd of mustangs galloping across the savanna. The shock as the lasso caught lifted me right off the ground and sat me astride a rather frisky mare that I recognised immediately. Aragon had done as I had and we galloped side by side towards a horizon of mountains the colour of goldfish. The goldfish were eating all the apples off the trees and we almost drowned trying to shoot them dead with our revolvers.

When I was quite sure that the bicarbonate astrologer was far away I dismounted. In spite of its whinnying I managed to get the mare to lie down. Amidst a flurry of bucking we ended up in a frightful embrace after getting into a tangle with each other. Aragon sang:

*A short telegraphist the omelette's flower has snapped*
*a typist in the office hid my gaze from view.*
*Do give me back my matches please, then I'll adapt*
*this stencil's plan to build the universe anew.*

*The sky we stuck with margarine*
*the image of our lusts and lewdest knocks*
*that makes three francs each magazine*
*as carnal pride is mostly sung in smocks.*

When I got up again the mare had been transformed. Miss Flowers was standing there before me.

She cried out:

"The flooding is laying waste to a neighbourhood affected by meningitis. A river has spun on the axis of two glances and the blessing of these skeletal silences will allow the redskin to impart his philosophical opinions."

Galloping off on Aragon's horse, she disappeared across the plains, not even turning round as we called after her.

Aragon then made me realise the state my clothes had fallen into, and sharply reprimanded me for not taking care of his embroidered armband. But all that was nothing more than a minor irritation in the palm of my hand. We sat in silence and when the sun struck twelve we didn't throw a single coin into the plate Louis Morin was holding out to us.

At four o'clock in the afternoon we roused ourselves. We had hardly walked a hundred metres when a strange sight met our eyes. Two phalluses, that we knew belonged to Louis Morin and the Captain and which were joined together at the testicles, were dancing about and talking. Up above, Benjamin Péret's arm was beating time. All in all it was a marvellous scene to behold.

This is what the two conjoined phalluses were saying:

> *Heed not, I say, the barrister carafe*
> *if I show you the path again*
> *from brothel to the champagne's telegraph*
> *and flagging north wind takes the train*
>
> *I do not know the Marquis's hole*
> *Old Corsican, it's time to die*
> *the head of Barrès whence we stole*
> *a sob, with laughter wheeling by*

*Tsar Nicholas out on the terrace stood*
*'midst bread and chickweed there for painters' scams*
*three lovers in the corner of a wood*
*a snipe that turns all virgins into jams.*

When they had stopped, Benjamin Péret's arm turned a small crank that was protruding from between the testicles. Immediately they took up again, even more sweetly than before:

*The nervous doorbell lets its muscles rest*
*It's Victor foxtrot, small old man with valves*
*God save the smoke of virgin monkey-puzzles*
*Your titties' tips by train tongues soon are salved.*

*Messrs de Goncourt go to the cinematic Bible*
*to bring justice to the petty thief*
*who was turning the cranks*
*that will fill 244 litres.*

We could have carried on listening to this charming little song for a long time if Verdure had not come by. I stood up.

"What are you going to do?" asked Aragon.

"Make love," I answered.

"But he's a man."

"Man or woman, it makes no difference. The jewel I'm after is sealed within his quivering belly. I'm going to seek it out. I shall strangle the sun with my bare hands and the orange-flower gulfs can but curve their luxuriant backbones at the fulfilment of my love."

"What a mistake," Aragon said. "You have never liked raw onions or the sound of mirages."

Just then Benjamin Péret's arm grabbed the declaiming genitals and carried them off far away. We would never see any of them again.

Aragon departed as fast as he could on his roller skates. As he was leaving he knocked over a horde of redskins in mayflower. When he was no more than a speck in the distance, I turned and walked away. I must have walked the better part of that night.

## THE SINGING TAP

*A dish was dashed to death by vulture's flight*
*the same that put its wing around a quail*
*so lead inside my head would not be right*
*wide window, the quicksilver sings its scale*

*The snail of Burgundy that digs your graves*
*the cigarette end burns out in your gut*
*the accordion collapsing now in waves*
*knows destiny's syringe and nothing but*

*Tsar Nicholas out on his terrace stood*
*'midst bread and chickweed there for painters' scams*
*three lovers in the corner of the wood*
*a snipe that turns all virgins into jams.*

## TESTAMENT FOR MY FRIENDS

*Messrs de Goncourt go to the cinematic Bible*
*to bring justice to the petty thief*
*who was turning the cranks*
*that will fill 244 litres.*

## TREBLE CLEF

*The anaemia of cars*
*has the sound of open doors*
*the morals and the flour*
*of the man from Córdoba who moulds the discharge*
*from a cooker made of Bessarabian iron.*

## PRAYER

*The nervous doorbell lets its muscles rest*
*It's Victor foxtrot, small old man with valves*
*God save the smoke of virgin monkey-puzzles*
*Your titties' tips by train tongues soon are salved.*

## PHILOSOPHICAL CONTROVERSIES

*Ape not, I say, the barrister carafe*
*if I show you the path again*
*from brothel to the champagne's telegraph*
*and flagging north wind takes the train*

*I do not know the Marquis's hole*
*old Corsican, it's time to die*
*the head of Barrès whence we stole*
*a sob, with laughter wheeling by*

*You proverb, you are not all waters with their minerals*
*From touches of our songs we make our soles*
*and here too, grazing bulls in crystal bowls*
*On springs, the blind man on the secret stairs of stored quenelles.*

I made my way past two circular red and amber railways signals that were giving birth to strange flowers in the air. When I arrived, the pharmacy door swung open by itself. Behind the counter, Paul Smara was busy conjugating a verb in order to bring Isabeau of Bavaria back to life. Jars lined all the shelves. Twelve of them contained a blue light-bulb. Twelve of them each contained three fingers writhing about in all directions at once. One of the jars appeared to be empty.

"Can I help you?" Paul Smara asked.

"I'll have that jar."

"The smoke-blackened pyramid and the collapse of chromatic corpuscles, it's because of these that I've failed. Take this jar if it makes you happy. After all, your fate means nothing to me."

I grabbed hold of the jar I coveted. As I did so, the lid flew off up into the air, saying:

"I am Guillaume Apollinaire."

Immediately I felt paralysed, blind and dumb all the way down my left side. I quickly realised that it was simply because my body had split in two from my head down to my toes. The other half was standing in front of me. The cross-section of my body was glazed. I could tell this by the way my other half appeared. Through the shop window I watched as various numbers continuously wove in and out of each other. There were four bees flying around a poppy, which I could see was a lung. Almost in the middle of it all was an electric switch. To my great surprise my other half spoke in the following terms:

"I, Guillaume Apollinaire, take from you this portion of your body, for you owe it to me. The Sacré-Cœur exults when it invokes the pea-flower. Delaunay, the painter, has crucified me on the Eiffel Tower but as a tribute this weighs on me. I arrived here on a train of Hertzian waves. The express trains that run over your body without hurting you have the flavour of bananas. Prolegomena and postulates will do you no harm and the pregnant guard will multiply the garrison's desires. Come."

And off we hopped. We made a pile of money playing hopscotch with the children of billionaires, and women lying in confinement spontaneously gave birth while we watched to mysterious equations that sang the glory of the poet of *Calligrammes*. Unfortunately, the beloved host of my other half-body got caught in a wolf trap. He was immediately transformed into telegraph wires.

And there it is. I have told you the secret. Every telegraph wire is none other than Apollinaire. It was also there that he wrote that wonderful song without a single note between its lines. The very song that's gone right round the world. As for me, I returned to my previous form. A step ladder appeared; I climbed it so that I could whisper the secrets of the savanna to the soul of Croniamantal. Unfortunately it didn't reach high enough and I was obliged to climb back down again. But instead of coming down headfirst I came down backwards, which meant that I didn't know when I had arrived at ground level and so I continued downwards. I realised my mistake too late. I was heading for the fire in the centre of the Earth.

I found myself in a large room in which several funnels were bumping into each other in a harmonious din. Fearlessly I walked across the room. In the middle was a small basin in which a celluloid duck was bobbing about.

I continued on my journey. Miss Flowers held out her hand so that we could step out into the fresh air and then told me the following:

"A dirigible was manœuvring over the city. People live there who are really only spheres with five rotating arms and legs. Some of them were sinking down while they spun around. Then jets of fire spurted from the mouths of the sewers for no reason, cathedral organs began trumpeting the horror of perfumes in prison and metal slugs were slithering along the walls… Distraught, I confided my fear to Apollinaire's soul."

"What did he say?"

"He told me, 'Worse is not a pejorative.'"

"'Pontius Pilate is not an example of universal gravitation.'"

"'In the corridors of Hell there are corners where the light from your cigarettes hides after they have gone out.'"

I felt considerably baffled at this. A motorised dinghy was moored there, ready to go. We jumped in and left.

Hands emerged from the Seine. Some were holding bottles and inside one I found this message:

> *Fire's hope is rich and bright*
> *the perfume of beloved martyrs*
> *exhales, but oh so slight*
> *the flag that at Palmyra flutters.*
>
> *So fan yourselves with your kerchiefs*
> *or else tonight we die*
> *and in the towns so long besieged*
> *light-hearted children lie*
> *and tell of the absurd adventure*
> *the nightingale and Kurdish warrior.*

What could we do? Miss Flowers and I took out our handkerchiefs. Lone horsemen, there on the riverbank, mistook them for targets. Not one of their bullets hit us, but they made holes in the sky at our eye-level. From behind a clump of elms a series of bugle calls rang out. The flag of an invisible standard flapped like an exploding artillery shell. Clouds took on the shape of unfamiliar flowers. The motorised dinghy raced on towards the sea. A small triangular flag fluttered in its wake. The current increased our speed still further. There were corpses floating close to the riverbed. As we passed it I recognised what was without any doubt the corpse of Benjamin Péret. Further on we saw a man swimming against the current. He greeted us as we passed by with these words:

"The solidified water at the poles is the hope of ideal fiancées. At the ball, confetti will ring out with loud fanfares. Asiatic warriors dressed in silk and feathers will fix yours to the walls with silver pins. The flowers will die without butterflies. Hurry on to the high seas! It is the scent of death that draws me to these places. Dreadful things are going to happen! Flee!"

"I know that swimmer," said my companion, seated beside me, after the man had moved on. "One day I saw him walking down the street, making no sound. Suddenly he turned towards me, pointed to a coachman who was quietly minding his own business, and said, 'That man is going to die.' Blazing stars fell from the sky on to the rooftops, the rooftops in the street. Once everything had calmed down again, I saw that the man had disappeared. The coachman was dead."

Busy as I was with examining the mystery that was our other companion, I kept my counsel. Soon after, the sea appeared. The pebbles on the shore were the skulls of the dead, rolled back and forth by the waves without shattering. The lighthouses waved their arms in the mist at flotillas whose black gables, topped with flags, stood out against the horizon. The dinghy headed towards them. Masses of people dangled in silence from the rope-ladders. The captain stood with one foot on the bridge of each warship. Perched atop the highest mast, a cabin-boy was singing:

> *I see the towers of Notre Dame,*
> *the clarions of Jericho*
> *this crowd I'm starving isn't calm*
> *they lost their gold in Monaco.*

With difficulty we navigated the eighteen rows of dwarfs who were encircling us. Some of them gestured in our direction, their porthole eyelids blinking one by one. Several leagues further on we encountered a lone vessel, the last of the fleet, racing full steam ahead to catch up with the others. Vitrac was standing at the stern. With his hair he was pulling naked swimmers from all the recesses in the waves while friendly porpoises were leaping around the propeller just like affectionate dogs.

We reached the open sea: no shore no birds no current. The dinghy stopped of its own accord.

"Do you remember the name of the steamer Vitrac was aboard?" Flowers asked.

"The *St Gildas's Cockerels,*" I replied.

"And the first one we encountered?"

"The *Frenetic Compass.*"

"I am as surprised at your reticence as I am at this blossoming of stars in the watery depths."

I looked. The sky was dark, but from the bottom of the sea glimmers of light were rising up, becoming brighter by the minute. Soon the light was dazzling! The shadow of our dinghy was projected on to the clouds hanging over us. Fish, with electric eyes which lit up the shallows, appeared at the surface of the waves and emerged from the sea and, with the steady, straight and silent flight of dirigibles, headed for land. A whale was gently pitching from side to side. For a long time a sea serpent sustained the gleam of its damp scales. Giant crabs, their claws outstretched, floated by in the air with mute resignation in the corners of their drooling mouths.

Then everything was desert.

When the waters started to recede, trees and coral appeared, the sea deserted the islands like gums pulled away from their teeth, and all was dry. On the sand I saw a small box. I opened it. Glittering inside were the diamonds and pearls Miss Flowers had been chasing after for so long. She seemed unsurprised. She twined them around her hips and neck and stood waiting for us anxiously.

In the sky the clouds were being torn apart as they were driven on by a fleet wind. Now and again as they bolted the moon appeared, with the result that it seemed to be spinning along at a dizzying speed. When the sky was clear and filled with stars, we could distinctly make out a number of flotillas climbing into the sky, as if ascending an invisible spiral staircase. Fish followed, and after them birds. Swallows twittered, their appearance preceding the sea-birds and raptors; others flew around, pell-mell. With their hides swaying from side to side, elephants led the procession of animals. They trumpeted their astonishing proclamations to all the worlds. Then there was order and calm once more.

The pearly ribbons of rapids in the hemispheres, the rolling of the great pipes, the precise gearing of unfamiliar vocabularies, all constituted, from this moment on, the very *raison d'être* for crimes. Young boys standing at level crossings invited travellers to alight. Those who did so were dragged by their feet to the nearest swamp. Mathematicians' set squares brought about worldwide catastrophes, the terrifying accounts of which were transmitted by trees all the way to the equator. Naked, gaunt and devastated, women waited at every milestone, thighs spread, sex. Negros, their noses pierced with gold hoops, took frenzied dancers prisoner. In deserted barracks drums beat the reveille endlessly, while at the same time cavalry trumpets sounded that the fires had been put out. Bottles changed shape. Priests worshipped gods nailed to five-pointed stars. Children born at this time all had navels that stuck out, instead of going in. Adolescents had dreams that were abstract nightmares similar to the life of the number 244 in the series of equations of some algebraic proof or other. Astronomers observed luminous signals in the starless skies. Children freely chose to die for no reason, old people prolonged their lives by means of intravenous injections which made the veins at the tops of their noses stand out, as well as those at their temples and around their ankles. Mr and Mrs Josephson and Malkine appeared on a path coming down a hill. Their arrival brought everything back to normal.

Baby elephants ate bars of chocolate out of Mrs Josephson's hand. Her husband watched as the street-lamps and flagpoles leaned down towards him.

As for Malkine, he was watching from the top of the headland as the tide rose in silence. The sea serpent prowled around him for a long while before taking up its sleeping position again somewhere near the Marquesas Islands.

Slow, majestic waves lifted our dinghy, the motor started purring again and the propeller beat against the water.

Standing at the prow of the boat, Miss Flowers exclaimed, "Who is it who makes flowers bloom in the lungs of consumptives?

"Who is it who destroys the equilibrium of diaphragms?

"Who is it who, in one movement, lowers the cannons and semaphores towards the rivers?

"Who is it who drowns without mercy the pupils of the eyes in alphabetic memories?

"Who? Who? He alone will be my lover."

And the dinghy continued on its way while the moon rose slowly above us out of a luminous and inexplicable question-mark.

Mineral foliage fermented drinks, our nights of love looked just like you. The fragrant algae overshadowing us has left the reflection of swift meridians on our foreheads. The passing hours felt like vertigo at high altitudes. On which blackboard did I write the relationship between heart and hands, and the formula for unsuspected carbide? Roll on, you fiery dancing circles and rain-sodden boulevards. Motorised candles were making tumultuous waves and the submerged towns held up their rusting engines to the sky. Carabineers and advance scouts suffocated when the searchlight swept across the countryside. Crippled old men, just before losing their very last teeth, uttered words that plunged their sons into horror and devastation. Anglers were dragged along in the wake of powerful fish. Lightning streaked the sky without a sound.

The dinghy stopped right in the middle of a harbour. A new jetty extended on one side, with a small red-brick lighthouse at the end. The town was composed of streets laid out in perfectly straight lines that intersected at right angles. Policemen* stood at every corner. A cosmopolitan crowd, made up of whites, blacks and Asiatics, was hurrying along without talking. Even the cars made no noise, at most letting slip the occasional whistle. In a theatre we were present as a baby was delivered. Eighteen dwarfs on kazoos accompanied the birth. That evening, women came to us. Miss Flowers stared at them out of curiosity. They glanced at the state of our fingernails and left. In a café the Captain, Verdure and Baignoire were drinking whisky. We went in and sat down at their table.

"Have you found your jewels?" asked the officer, growing pale.

"Yes," said Miss Flowers, "and I also found this at the bottom of the sea."

Verdure, Baignoire and I let out a cry. In her hand she held a radium compass with two needles. The Captain examined it.

"This needle," he said, "is pointing to the South Pole, but the other one is pointing in an unknown direction."

"That is the one we are following."

"On your way you will meet jockeys with no names. The bucking of their horses will bring forth armies of Samurai clad in bronze."

"They're already here," the American woman said.

We stood up.

Marching down the street came an army of Chinese soldiers. They were wearing check suits and were armed with revolvers, and each of them held a phonograph horn in his right hand. Their lifeless eyes resembled those of the blind.

A strange music came after them. The crowd gathered on the pavement was making exaggerated gestures, devoid of any meaning.

Miss Flowers said to me:

"Don't you think that the blood of young girls flows more quickly in the middle of the river? The hinges of trick boxes shatter at my glance. The thing we are waiting for is about to happen."

From behind an open-work wooden screen a woman appeared. In her hand she held a vaporiser. A spray of blue liquid refreshed our faces.

A great plain opened up before us. Our companions had disappeared. Around us, it was entirely deserted. We could barely make out the very top of the Eiffel Tower on the horizon. Something was glittering there, a mirror or some kind of metallic surface. Above it a flag was fluttering.

I was in the Place du Havre. For me, the Gare Saint-Lazare was nothing but a pile of green and red confetti from which flocks of birds were intoning the litanies of Mary:

"Holy Virgin, have pity on she who is not, or rather pity her not, nor grant her justice, but grant power for rent boys and prostitutes to reign over this imbecilic people."

Miss Flowers then burst out of a manhole. A child standing in the middle of the square was scaring the cars. At last the harbour opened out before us. Between two mooring bays floated the heads of several generals of the Republic. Flowers fished one out with her parasol: it was Hoche's head. The fishermen on the quay were kneeling in a circle around her, masturbating in a steady rhythm. Their wives presented a curious tableau. One woman's head was stuffed completely inside another woman's vagina, and they whirled around each other like spinning tops.

But now the Pantheon was opening up before us. Ministers in white bartenders' jackets were cutting off the limbs of important men. Hoche's head was auctioned off for 3 francs 50. Some English women purchased the viscera of Victor Hugo very cheaply and Sadi Carnot's penis was the object of an astonishing bidding war between some gaily coloured homosexuals and Mr Nobel.

Finally we left. Here was the cathedral where once the phallus had foretold terrible things to me. In place of the door to the tabernacle was a red railway signal.

The train trundled over the arches making a tremendous noise and behind it snails slithered along quickly, leaving a silvery trail on the railway tracks and on women's bracelets.

Some priests appeared. They had votive candles burning in their flies, and their shafts stiffened in my direction. Taking refuge on top of the altar, I tore down the crucifix and used it to defend myself with mighty thrusts. When the chancel was strewn with the priests' broken skulls, I stopped. The wine in the chalice was a lovely garnet colour. On its label was the word *quinquina*. I drank it down in a single gulp.

Next I unscrewed the head of Christ from my improvised sword. It was the shaft of a key. The moment I removed the head, I saw that the penis of the sculpted god had disappeared and that in its place was the end of the key. I switched off the alarm on the tabernacle signal and took out Miss Flowers's necklace.

The crowd, who had been watching the scene on their knees, with their skirts, trousers and undergarments hitched up so that their naked skin was touching the tiles, all stood up as one. I realised that the necklace was thousands of kilometres long. The crowd helped me carry it and so it was that the sun, pierced by seventeen knives of different colours, witnessed me dragging the universe behind me, a slobbering Tarasque* with a gemstone spine.

On the white bellies of the women were tattooed the different parts of the world:

"Africa America Asia Oceania Europe
Greetings!
The breasts of my future wet-nurses
With your sunlit gulfs
And your poles in their eyes"

*O liners, liners, born of hearts of whales*
*sink not at last beneath our memories' swells*
*if four black horses when their breath exhales*
*should raise the fair's alarm that marks farewells*

# The Punishments of Hell

*The captain of the lovely* Eugénie
*Within his phonograph insulted comets*
*Three swimmers: kings of the epiphany*
*who brought the sleeping foetus*
*incense in a jar of alcohol between two epaulettes*

*The man with the pestle of marble pride's not me*
*The tenor marshals all with storms bedecked*
*whilst singing licked the statues' sexual parts*
*but at the fish feast died from bones unchecked*
*which pierced their eyes their hearts and navels too*

*The loves of nebulae, Oh, breasts of my mistresses!*
*Astronomers whose eyes out of their glasses popped*
*and these eyes in the skies like the eyes of negresses*
*my head and lusts reflected in their curves aloft.*

The rooftops of the houses were now the centre of concentric masked balls at which my heartbeats wept.

My name, written a hundred and four times on the walls, formed into the shape of the arrow I love. Arrows in the direction of multiple trains for the coast from which transoceanic bridges make their escape.

Their arcs became ellipses for a moment, thanks to their

reflections in the water, and English lancers in red jackets begged me to love them.

I know how a fire starts and I know how to solve quadratic equations and your spines supply my knucklebones, my lovely game of knucklebones.

With the linen cravat I wear I killed the king of England. Prince Pigalle gave me his daughter in marriage and I love the woman's hand that wins at poker.

Boys' hearts leapt silently on to the crystal blades of the parquet, the shape of a woman appeared on each one and I unlocked a hundred and forty-three doors with a single glance. A hundred and forty-three women stepped out. They wore green wigs and their knocking knees provided the beat for a dance between a snake and a tortoise.

Miss Flowers laid her hand on my shoulder.

"Your five-corners-of-the-world-at-a-hundred-and-eighty-degrees eyes I will eat them."

She sank her teeth into my eye sockets. I felt the aqueous humour seeping into my gums.

When she unclenched her kiss new eyes grew back, green ones. Twenty times she gulped down my eyeballs, and twenty times green eyes were reborn in my sockets and I could only laugh. Her peacock-tail hair revealed thirty-seven discrete universes.

Miss Flowers lifted up her skirts.

Her vagina, Africa, O Africa, where the equator bloomed, opened up like a gorgeous flower. I lay down inside to rest. Rock-a-bye baby, sleep and pleasure, the love of two lovers nourished by each other's gazes. The two needles of the compass turned on the pivot of her navel and its W pole was the muscular arsehole into which my fingers disappeared. Her breasts were within reach of my mouth my teeth coupled with her milky nipples. With these two phalluses between my teeth, I dragged down three constellations with me and Amazonian rivers poured from my armpits.

Four aeroplanes were flying over the city. They shot out bursts of flame. Eighteen parachutes swung out into the void between the four columns of fire. When they were near the ground I could see they were eighteen women wearing full skirts. Where each of their arms should have been propellers whirred. They landed softly. A golden anchor hung from each of their belts and their long blue hair sank the sloops and drowned all their crews.

The crowd, however, was swallowing the necklace. When each person had swallowed a stone they were turned into pills. An invisible genie put them into jars on the glass shelves in the pharmacy. In my hand I held only Miss Flowers's hand.

"Do you think," she said, "that I've at last escaped my pursuers? No!"

"What else can they do?" I asked.

"Look."

A group of bandits in the pay of the Captain had surrounded us. We had to run and take cover in the pharmacy.

The shots fired from their revolvers shattered the bottles of perfumed liquid.

"In the unstable solution where my descendants swim about," I said, "there's enough room for several cities."

"That's exactly what's at stake here," she replied, and she was right.

Our ammunition had run out... Already our assailants were scrambling up the mound of bodies formed of those we had killed. The Seine is a tranquil river but when it is possessed by the wrath of God or by the elements it can, in a single torrent, leap from its bed, sweep away the bridges, smash into the walls of the Louvre and the Palais de Justice and, more effectively than lightning, fire, cannon shells or the hands of men, carry off monuments and miscreants in its vengeful waters.

While all this was going on the Seine was indeed slowly rising, right up to the steps of the quays, and soon the landing-stages were just specks on the horizon. The barges were long gone, carried off beyond Le Havre.

Behind a blue jar in the window I caught sight of the head of one of the bandits. Seizing a spinal needle used for making lumbar punctures I plunged it into his heart. Blood spurted right up to the electric lights and we were bathed in red.

The water was gaining ground. The Louvre was dissolving. Paintings were being swept off all the way to the Americas and the marble statues were being sucked down into the silt. The Rue de Rivoli was a torrent in flood, and the waters rushed down the Rue Notre-Dame-de-Lorette. After a long while Monsieur Louis de Gonzague-Frick floated up to the surface. His eye, a white headlamp, reflected the sun all the way to the horizon, one arm called the void to witness, and that was it for Monsieur Louis de Gonzague-Frick. Suddenly the door of the pharmacy gave way under the weight of our attackers. The last of the jars then shattered a few more skulls. Someone's hand was clutching Miss Flowers by the neck. I put my hand on her shoulder. Her head turned to face me. I did not recognise her.

A violent punch sent me tumbling to the ground, and I passed out. I was brought to my senses again by water entering my nostrils. There were two feet splashing around within hand's reach, and I grabbed them. The man fell, and sitting on the back of his neck I waited until he had drowned.

We were saved. Flowers fell into my arms.

The water was up to our hips. We escaped it by jumping from one shelf to another. But the waters were rising, and kept on rising. The ceiling prevented us from climbing any higher. Was this how we were going to die, a pair of Cartesian divers with no way out? My hand alighted on something round. I moved towards a small oval window already being lapped at by the water. Saved! We were saved. They were oxygen tanks. Quickly we made our escape, after I had checked the time on the clock on the wall. It was a quarter past three.

Outside the sun was shining. We turned round and the oval window was already submerged and gone. I thought I saw a boat in the distance. It was the top of the Arc de Triomphe. Moments later and that too was lost from view. Shouts! André Breton was standing on the bow of a rowing-boat. He helped me on board. But Miss Flowers turned away.

We watched as she left, buoyed up by two massive testicles, in the direction of a bleeding anus on the horizon that was swallowing up the waves, the stars and the night. I looked at the time. It was eight twenty-five in the evening.

"Was it such a long time ago," I asked André Breton, "that the jets of water spurted all over our national history?"

"It was six days ago."

"And now the labyrinth of corridors traced out by my life in the atmosphere is producing the heartbeats of a resonant and metallic world!"

"Yes, but look!"

The waters were roaring away to the west at the speed of a fast-flowing river. Soon we had come to rest on silty ground. Miss Flowers sped past us like a mustang at the gallop.

"The waters are rushing around the Earth from east to west at the same speed as a twenty-four hour round-the-world trip. Run, or the incoming tide from the east will drown you!"

At that, our feet sprang on to the motorcycle foot-rests.

"What time is it?" I asked André Breton.

"Ten past eight."

We sped off. Whole trains that had come off the rails were chasing after the ebbing waters so as to escape the seas that had become one when the tide turned. Enormous locomotives with bloodshot eyes were lowing. Cars chased after each other with their desperate klaxons, and the global population was on the move all over the world. Oh, those people halted by exhaustion! And those whom sorrows forced to lie down and rest beside the tombs of the prejudiced! The water drowned them all, unmourned and unloved.

Tremble, ye nations upon nations! In vain do your flags imitate the waves, though winkles and mussels cling to your flagpoles. Where are your national glories and where is your outmoded pride? Where are your deathly vanities, their colourful fins full of holes like doughty battle pennants? All mere flotsam and jetsam at the mercy of tropical storms and the equatorial current.

The statues of your great men? The temples where your flags crystallise into funerary golds? The tombs of your generals, your philanthropists and philatelists? Reefs, reefs, reefs! on which steamships sailing out of control are wrecked. The wave toys for a moment with luxuriant thighs, and new-born babies are impaled on cathedral spires six hundred metres below the surface! We spied them when, our feet weighed down by silt, we were chasing the waves in the company of some pleasant crabs, amongst the glinting of fish out of water as they leapt in and out of deoxygenated pools. And your laws and mottos? That's where the octopuses and lobsters that kill each other find reasons for hope! The seaweed snags on the parapets of the transoceanic bridges we cross once a day. The city of Ys?* I passed through it one day. Oculists' shops amounting to two hundred in number were all lit up there. Artificial eyes of all colours glittered in their boxes, oh clairvoyant jewels, and the inhabitants, immunised against drowning, sneered and laughed at us as they watched us pass.

"What time is it, André Breton?"

"It's ten past eight."

"Again!"

As we passed by the urinals in the street the noise made by the typewriters was terrifying, and luminous sentences described surprising parabolas in the clouds sprinkled with rainbows and aurorae borealis.

"What time is it, André Breton?"

"It's ten past eight."

An aeroplane took us on a journey that lasted a week. The lines of cars and locomotives hauling train carriages by the hundred made for a tragic spectacle.

Those who had taken refuge in the high mountains had seen the glaciers melting into salt water; then, the undertow had caused the rocky peaks to crumble and processions of corpses marked the parallels of latitude and the direction of the sun's progress.

"What time is it, André Breton?"

"It's ten past eight."

Octopuses left behind in the water-holes attacked the refugees. Hundreds of people bogged down in the mud were drowned but still the sun was projecting our shadows the same way as usual on to the ground.

"What time is it, André Breton?"

"It's ten past eight."

Straight after we landed we bumped into Madame Breton. She was wearing a necklace of shells and Harry the baby marmoset was perched on her shoulder, playing a kazoo. The three of us pressed on with our escape. Some of those who had embarked in submarines found themselves sinking into the ground and the fire in the centre of the Earth liquefied their watertight hulls. Those who were left behind in the rush awaited death in hideous acts of love, and the milky atolls they could make out at the surface of the waves gave the illusion of swimmers in trouble.

SUDDENLY THE SEA STOPPED!

But only for a moment! It started to roil again but this time from west to east. Night followed day twice as fast as usual. We held on to the touching memory of the perpetual morning that had lit up the last few days.

The sliver of crescent moon in the sky, the support for our mappa mundi globe, had slipped away, quite mad. For several hours we fled in the company of a regiment of firemen. Their sirens called endlessly for the fire that was their saviour and they threw off their helmets like so much cumbersome ballast. The helmets lay scattered along our path for some time. The clouds drew on them the parts of the world that were underwater and seahorses died for want of admiring themselves in their shiny surfaces.

Millions of Chinese were running past with their arms held tight to their sides. Cannons gorged on this tide by their breech and then spat out… the grotesque hoarded figurines with their muzzles stretched wide.

The liners, submerged for long years with their stolen treasures, were stopping for no one. At a bend along the peninsula I found myself alone. I managed to keep sight of Aragon for a few hours but then he too was gone from view. Baron, Vitrac and Morise passed within range of my voice but I couldn't catch up with them. For four days Miss

Flowers gave me starry nourishment from her milky breasts. The volcanoes spewed out cinders and lava but to no effect. They alternated between being extinct and being active. Such petty matters then were our beliefs, religions and sense of decency. All that mattered was the safety of the individual and no one disputed that. Entire oyster beds decorated the relics of vanity while astronomers on neighbouring planets noted the existence of a blue ring encircling the Earth like the blade of a sabre.

It was an uninterrupted convoy of aeroplanes whose propellers whirred with the rhythm of heroic eulogies. Presidents of Republics! Kings! Grocers! Bald men, we have awarded your laurel wreaths to the school student who won first prize in gymnastics, while your brains, those sponges engorged with water, piss out through your glaucous eyeballs.

Eventually, after thirty-four days of life carrying on like this, the oceans and rivers packed themselves off to their beds. Naked female bathers swam about in full view of the fashionable beaches, women lifted up their skirts in my presence and everything was just as it used to be.

Louis Aragon said:

"Our bodies make an everlasting matrix in the air around us. The trace of your movements is invisible but lives on for ever in space. I have found a way of casting this in bronze."

He stopped in front of a tree.

"Here," he said, "right here is where Arthur Rimbaud once stood for ten minutes. Look."

Liquid bronze poured from a petrol can. Before long it had formed into a statue with a hundred and forty-three arms, seventy-nine legs and a monstrous head pocked with three thousand and four eyes, fifty-eight burning foreheads and eighty-four mouths agape.

I looked at Aragon.

"What you have cast is a statue not of Rimbaud but of all those who have ever stopped here, one single statue representing all the people who have stopped here. Oh, cursed be the dead, or rather, let us know nothing of them. Only the living are beautiful and in the present, not in the past. I have two arms, two legs, two eyes and a mouth, I am fully capable of making love and my contempt is boundless for those who no longer can.

"Oh monstrous statue, that embodies all my misgivings and prejudices, I repudiate you. I had thought you were alive, quick-moving and handsome enough to be loved with sensual delight! But your tentacular arms are fixed, absurdly, in one position, your mouth is cold and suckerless and your limbs do not experience the slightest spasm! I hate them.

"And you, whom I called to mind at the climax of my masturbations: Rimbaud, Apollinaire, Lautréamont, Jarry, Jacques Vaché — you smell bad, you are all ugly, you are incapable of making or thinking about love, you are dead!

"YOU ARE DEAD! YOU ARE DEAD!"

Who are Rimbaud, Apollinaire, Lautréamont, Jarry and Jacques Vaché? These names remind me of the names of flavours from long ago, but I have quite forgotten what they refer to!

So it is that when a trapper meets a tribe of Indians on the warpath, his first instinct is to try and hide behind some rocks or bushes. He lies down flat on the ground, slinking around them so that the wind carries his scent away in the other direction, climbing, invisible to the untrained eye, making sure not to bend the grass, muffling the very beating of his heart, dimming the flash of his eyes, even as, listening intently, he watches with a piercing gaze, and gathers the sounds and movements of the landscape. A fox gets up as he approaches; he could easily grab it but its rare and silky pelt holds little interest for him. He lets it escape. He discards the valuable otter-skins he is carrying in his game-bag, because they are slowing him down. He keeps only his Winchester rifle and continues with his escape. He steps right into a nest of loathsome snakes. He pays no heed to them. One of them slides in through an opening in his shirt and settles itself against his stomach. He doesn't even twitch at the deathly cold of its scales. The cruel snake gives him a vicious bite on the navel. There is not so much as a twitch in his little toe. Blood trickles down his body into his groin, which is equally impassive. He bears the pain until the reptile, vanquished by such heroic courage, slowly slips out and rejoins its fellows in the darkness of the damp undergrowth.

But what good is all this heroism? The Indians' prairie dogs have caught his scent, the moon rises swiftly and casts his shadow and a scout gives a guttural cry. And now the whole tribe is in pursuit of the ill-fated man. With the eight bullets in his rifle he kills eight Indians, but there are a hundred more behind them. He runs. There is a canyon up ahead of him, he can hide there in the convenient pools of darkness amongst the rocks. Too late: a Sioux look-out has spotted him. He retraces his steps, evades his pursuers even as he rushes to meet them, and enters their camp, sowing panic amongst the women and spreading fire through the tents, which blaze up brightly. The flames attract the men who are chasing him, but dashing into the horse enclosure he cuts the reins tethering them with a few slashes of his Bowie knife, leaps astride one of the horses and gallops off with the rest of the horses behind him. Will he get away? Arrows whistle all around him, shooting into the ground. This is exactly how the battle of Poitiers with King John and his son is represented in French history books in schools. Look to the left, trapper, look to the right! He gallops faster, he is out of arrow-shot, but not, alas, beyond the range of the chief's rifle, standing in his eagle-feather head-dress. A bullet hits the belly of the mustang he's riding and they both crash to the ground. He's going to get caught — but not yet.

One of the mares, thrown into a panic by the Indians' cries, brushes right past him. He grabs her tail and leaps on to her back. Is he really going to get away? Yes. No. Some of the Indians have managed to grab two or three of their horses, and off they gallop. Three lassos whistle and the trapper is caught by three nooses and yanked into the grass. His Bowie knife was still sheathed in one of the gaiters that covered the whole length of his legs; he cuts one of the lassos, then cuts a second. But, half-strangled, his energy is fading. He is unable to free himself from the third.

When he comes to, he finds himself lashed to a stake. The Sioux are walking round him with silent steps, treading first with the tips of their toes. They are chanting:

> *My toe following in the tracks of your toe*
> *brave companion*
> *and the shadow of my eagle and vulture feathers*
> *following in the shadow of your eagle and vulture feathers*
> *and my breath*
> *following in the tracks of your breath's canoe*

> > *Let us thrust our lances*
> > *into the flanks of brown mares*
> > *tossing their beautiful brown manes*
> > *skyward at our lunges*

The eyes of our squaws
are two cuts made by a tomahawk
the patterns on the shell of the great turtle
are not as beautiful
as our war tattoos

Let us thrust our lances
into the flanks of brown mares
tossing their beautiful brown manes
skyward at our lunges

Our eyes gleam
like the corn silk cigarettes smoked by the Spanish settlers
our pipe transports us to the land of peace and war
faster and further
than the whirring beast of the pale-faces
that climbs the ladder
to the point in the sky
where the evening sun glows

Let us thrust our lances
into the flanks of brown mares
tossing their beautiful brown manes
skyward at our lunges

*Sometimes we attack him*
*by the beaver's fur, the trappers' fortune*
*beautiful mulatto women swoon in our arms*
*on their chests we place our moccasins*
*but we love none but our own squaws*

> *Let us thrust our lances*
> *into the flanks of brown mares*
> *tossing their beautiful brown manes*
> *skyward at our lunges*

> *And we scalp*
> *we scalp the beautiful mulatto women*
> *we scalp the trappers*
> *and the wagon-drivers*
> *Let us sing, brave companion*
> *and drink the fire water*

When he comes to, there is a general howling and whirling and dancing, and the braves are circling around their victim. Tomahawks fly through the air. As the wood catches light, will they split open the trapper's skull? No. Fifty tomahawks become embedded in the post he is tied to, only a few centimetres from his face. Three times the game begins anew. Then the women arrive. They force needles under his fingernails and bite his cheeks, thighs and hands. The men's dance begins again. This time slim daggers are thrust into his exposed chest, but only piercing his skin just enough for a trickle of blood to flow. Throughout it all, retaining his dignity, the trapper sings:

*St Sebastian was never so joyful*
*another tomahawk strikes*
*shearing off that part of my brain*
*where I was thinking about Kitty, the damn bitch*
*who cheated on me, but I took her virginity*

*Thirty-two stars on my flag*
*stars and stripes*
*smashed to pieces on the rails*
*under the hooves of their mustangs*
*I won't spit my tongue in their face*

*I want to shout I want to scream I want to sing*
*I want to live another ten minutes*
*of lyrical cowardice*
*through my words and the struggle*
*of seeing myself through their eyes*

*Another tomahawk strikes*
*in a fragment of my brain*
*that escapes in tatters*

*The Punishments of Hell*

*that's where the painting was*
*which belonged to Miss Flowers from San Francisco*

*Strike, strike, brave Comanches!*
*My breasts my genitals and gums!*
*My teeth strung in a necklace around lascivious throats!*
*My scalp hanging at your hip!*
*Your arses on my work-shy mares!*

*Stars of my flag stars and stripes*
*I care nothing for your colours*
*or your mottos*
*or your bankers in their vaults*
*Massachusetts Alaska Oregon*
*Missouri Mississippi New York*
*Kentucky*
*I regret nothing*
*Washington and Lafayette*
*Franklin nor my bicycle*
*nor the rifle with which I killed*
*a president of the republic!*

*Another tom—*

*Give me a drop of rum!*

Suddenly everything stops moving and the great Chief approaches, knife in hand. Thirty seconds later, the unfortunate man's scalp
is hanging from the end of the Chief's outstretched arm, *hurrah hurrah
hurrah,* and the circle dance starts up again and forty-nine blowpipe darts
become embedded all round his right eye and forty-nine more round his
left eye and a ninety-ninth pierces his right eyeball and a hundredth his
left eyeball. In vain did he try to close his eyes; the first darts had pinned
his eyelids to his cheeks and forehead. His navel is the bull's-eye of a
target bristling with sharpened darts and the dance continues.

Three miles away, cowboy James and his friends are driving their
herd of cows and bulls. The Sioux, absorbed in their revenge, haven't
placed any guards, and their singing reaches the youngest cowboy, who
is holding up the rear. He calls out for a long while to James, at the head
of the long column, James the leader, who is singing:

> *Oh valiant bull*
> *I wrestle by its horns to ground*
> *oh valiant horse*
> *on roads where milestones none are found*
> *ah, how intoxicating*
>
> *I prospected for gold*
> *I hunted beaver*

*and so I was called Burning Wood, keeper of the* manada*
*of Nevada*

*I was a trapper here*
*and the furry foxes*
*were caught in my traps*
*amidst the brush and rocksies*
*by a foot placed in fear*

*In Europe I'm a nobleman*
*but here I ride a horse*
*four fortunes through my hands have run*
*one at a time of course*
*I care nothing for my noble seat:*
*this herd of cattle I've got's the best*
*eighteen mares that get no rest*
*and each in turn I ride and ride*
*till they've got no going left inside*

*My carbine and my Smith & Wesson*
*have planted firm and true the flag*
*the stars and stripes in many a chest an'*
*in many a gambling man and lag*

"Say James, can you hear that cursèd singing?"

"Shoot, short-eared Bob, you think I'm deaf? I hear it."

The sixty boys rode up and gathered into a group, their rifles trained.

"Howdy, pardners, listen up!"

"To the death!" reply the fearless comrades.

They huddle into a confabulation then four of them go off to scout out the Redskins' camp.

While this is going on the others move the oxen and the bulls and the jittery cows on to a wide bridge. Someone lights a fire behind them. The bellowing herd charges, goaded on by these tough men. Is that the reflection of the fire over there on the other side of the plain? No, it must be a different one, or else what would the four fellows who just left have been up to?

The Indians have seen the danger, but too late. The herd tramples them and their women. The bellowing herd thunders over the children and the tents, and only comes to a stop when it reaches the second blaze. At which point the cattle turn back the way they came and continue their labour of destruction.

James and his gang wreak sickening carnage. Those who are not killed outright are burned to a cinder, and a dozen are taken prisoner. The gang wastes no time in slicing open their bellies, cutting off their genitals and stuffing them in their mouths, before cutting off their heads and cramming them inside their bellies.

At that moment they catch sight of the trapper tied to his post. He is still moving, but feebly, and begging for water. They flay him alive, and with great hoots of laughter watch him as he dies.

Meanwhile, the fire is getting closer.

The cowboys gather round and James ends his song of glory:

> *And in a hole upon the bank of a river wide*
> *my three new shirts and noble titles did I hide*
> *but my lasso, the finest necklace*
> *that death could ever hope to possess*
> *will carry on its strangling me for some time yet*
> *before I shall agree to leave this close thicket*
> *where dancing like a ram the sun is in the west.*

When the two fires, having joined together as one, died for want of fuel, there remained no trace of men or animals, alive or dead.

That's how I met Miss Flowers.

On 17 July 1916, I was crossing the bridge that connects the Morgue with the Ile Saint-Louis. A woman was walking ahead of me, wearing a dark-blue tailored suit with a darker-blue check. I had noticed earlier, on the square in front of Notre Dame, the exuberant swaying of her hips and rear. When she got to the bridge I mentioned before, she said to a police officer:

"Magistral humidity administered in huge doses does not justify the power wielded by lawyers. Hair weeps on the helms of ships in distress. The shells the hair has escaped from are mimicking the sound of cars. The nativity of the most holy Virgin bruised my breasts. Silence, voracious bird."

"Please, go ahead," replied the representative of the civil police.

At which the woman stepped over the parapet. Just as she dropped down into the void I caught a glimpse of a black mark on the fabric that nestled between white thighs trussed by elastic garters.

And all this time the policeman was singing a little song:

*You never knew how much I loved your eyes*
*Oh Maréchal de Gramont, bottled in your mountaineering*
*the wheels of Shackleton's ship with their rise*
*and rising hubs that crushed the fish that were most hard of hearing*

"Officer," I said, "I have a few things to say to you. This jacket (I shall take it off) contains my fortune. Look after it well. These trousers (I shall take them off), be most careful that no one steps on them because of the crease. These socks (I shall take them off) are made of silk. I paid eleven francs for them."

When I had finished, all my clothes lay on the ground except my shirt. The policeman drew his sword and stood to attention. I climbed over the parapet and jumped.

The mineral verdigris at the corners of my thoughts attributes the sun's heat to the gazes of passers-by.

As I swam I sang a dirty little song that I can no longer remember.

Just a few strokes ahead of me, the woman was struggling. I soon caught up with her. Her hat was in my hand and her chignon was coming undone. I dragged her by her red hair to a small flight of steps that descended below the level of the water. I climbed out with the river in my arms, the flowing river that stuck the shirt to my body. Four hundred women were studying me through the fabric. As for me, all I could see were the two canine teeth on either side of the mouth of the woman I had just rescued.

The crowd came down in silence to where I was standing. Two policemen walked towards me.

"What time is it?"

"It's in the cellar."

"And the fish?"

"It's with the needles stuck in the corks."

"Come along now."

Carrying the woman in my arms, I walked up the steps to the

quay. Four motorists wearing tortoiseshell glasses grabbed hold of me. I struggled, but in vain. They snatched my burden from my arms and, by the time I'd got back up on my feet, the apple-green car was disappearing around the corner of the Quai Saint-Louis. A sympathetic driver offered me a lift in his car, and, at top speed…

The following day, the police officer on duty between two and six in the morning at the foot of the steps in the Rue des Envierges noticed something in the shadows. It turned out to be four black smoking-jackets, their linings stained with fresh blood.

Understandably alarmed, the policeman rushed to the doctor, who plucked out the officer's right eye and the following morning the policeman was awarded a medal for life-saving.

Crouching on the front of the car, on the bonnet, I began communicating by means of illuminated signals with the woman I hoped to liberate. Using my hand, I alternately covered and uncovered the car's right headlight in such a way that I made letters in Morse code. She answered me by doing the same with her cigarette.

Eventually, around midday, we stopped at an inn. We ate together, fugitives and pursuers, at the same table, and then, as the clock struck two, the chase began again, wilder and more determined than before.

In the corridor of the train I bumped into one of the kidnappers. I lunged at his throat and his dentures flew out, right into my hand. I fled. Once I was alone in my compartment I placed the dentures on the seat and asked them:

"What colour is the sky?"

"C sharp."

"Temperature of his armpits?"

"Mineral."

"His name?"

Just as the dentures were about to answer they were smashed to smithereens by a bullet-shot from a revolver. Masked bandits were attacking the train. The windows cracked into perfect stars. Through one of them I saw the woman lying across the front of one of the horsemen's saddles.

I grabbed the horse by its tail, and at breakneck speed the three of us galloped off together. When the horseman slowed down from a gallop, he turned and held out his hand to me.

"Hey there, my friend."

"Hello."

"Fancy a game of poker?"

"Why not?"

By midnight I had won thirty thousand francs. The train was still moving. The stranger placed a hundred thousand-franc notes on the table.

"I'll stake that against whatever you want to bet."

We played our cards.

"Flush," he said.

I had a royal flush.

I noticed that the little images on his bank-notes showed the beautiful unknown woman.

The table began to spin round. Decapitated — with his head sitting in the middle of the table and his body the Devil knows where — the bandit had disappeared.

"Do you have a light?" she asked.

I handed it to her.

But what was it I wanted to ask her, I asked myself. I remembered the time she was in the bedroom. Her name! I didn't know her name. I went to bed. Soon after I realised that some of my enemies were releasing chloroform into the room through the keyhole.

There was a hole in the wall where a nail had been pulled out. I left through this hole as easily as if I were walking through a *porte cochère*.

When I returned the next morning I lay down, exhausted, on the bed. But the chloroform started hissing in my ears again. A *porte cochère* opened up in the wall. I left.

René Crevel, however, suddenly emerged from the chimney.

Miss Flowers was sitting on the ground. I sat down as well.

The airship broke free from the horizon and floated over the plain; five of its two-bladed propellers had come off. We soon realised that they were the strange creatures whose appearance had frightened my companion earlier. With the grace of freewheeling acrobats they made their way towards us, dropping gently to the ground.

> *Our names are Eusebius*
> *Clarinet Frilly-Stuff*
> *Synonym Torpedo*
> *if our appearance scares you*
> *don't get whooping cough*
> *we're going to tell you about some other*
> *supernumerary alkaloid doses*
> *that will make the ovoid lovers*
> *die of anchylosis.*

*Napoleon standing on the back of his horse again*
*feigns fireworks fuelled with petrol*
*and skating oxen in their bowls of porcelain*
*brought death to Sebastopol.*

*Britannicus in lemons' golden hollow*
*and the bitter whistling of the branches where the owls reside*
*my death in cotton wraps me, it's hard to swallow,*

*will tattoo the hemisphere with many a mahogany hillside.*

*André Breton, proclaiming a lighthouse to the tides' tunefulness,*
*brought the sail with its perforated corks into being*
*the bird adored by air and gearing*
*slowly calculates how the notes will progress.*

*With a glaze on his fingers Vitrac feels for the collodion*
*the coolness of a key in a humble corridor*
*the endless prayer whence is born our great pardon*
*at the bottom of steel lakes death committed before.*

*The war caravan that's equipped with cannon*
*puts thoughts of fires in fallow fields into everyone's head*
*and the serious problem solved by Aragon*
*which traces in the sky a diameter and its quaternary dread.*

Miss Flowers stood up.

"Bare head, bare feet, bare legs, bare brain, bare body, so that was the ideal of your faces on iodine tablets. What am I doing here, and in fact, what are you doing here? I will see you tonight, at the Pelican Bar. They've got cameras that can reproduce the features of imaginary characters. Be there."

She left.

At that moment the twenty-five clones of André Breton reappeared. They paraded in front of me, each one reciting a poem. I cannot remember every one. Here are a couple of them:

> *The unknown Moroccan is our reason for being*
> *with the semaphore friend of fires and rails*
> *near a solar disc by the metre's agreeing*
> *to create a thin-shouldered child of betrayals.*

> *Atop the high roofs an old piston and violin*
> *have chased off the blue sky born of a shirt*
> *our vows will set fire to the last of your kings*
> *and in your hand the fire of our hands has stirred.*

And then, with a gust of wind, they disappeared. Beings with five arms and five legs began twirling around me. I headed for the Eiffel Tower. At the entrance to Paris I saw that the customs officers had been beheaded. Their heads had been impaled on spikes beside the city gates. Down a side street I saw once more the Chinese army marching past. Accompanied by the strange beings, I drove towards the Chinese soldiers at an insane speed. We soon drew level, and I followed after them. They all entered a bathhouse. Coming from the booths I could hear the officers' commands and also some sailors' sea shanties:

*It's portside that wins, that wins*
*It's portside that wins over starboard*
*It's starboard that wins, that wins…*

alongside the creaking of the mooring ropes against their bronze posts.

I went into one of the rooms. The bath was filled with blue water. I got in and lay down. The taps murmured an account of a horrific crime that had taken place by the fireside. Those who were listening trembled with fear. A little girl had fallen into the flames. She burned to to death, and no one had noticed.

And then the giant balloon emerged from the drain in the gutter. With just one bounce it floated off over the rooftops. Its gondola was made of wicker. I wanted to see what time it was. I saw that my watch had been replaced by the inexplicable compass Miss Flowers had discovered. The balloon was heading swiftly in the unknown direction indicated by the compass's extra needle. I noticed that this needle was able to move freely and furthermore that it did not keep a constant angle with the one pointing north. I looked down at the ground. André Breton shook his fists twenty-five times at the new buildings. On the horizon, Tristan Tzara was walking on his hands. The helicoidal figures were rushing towards the earth. In the distance, over the Eiffel Tower, the mysterious dirigible was changing course. I watched my balloon. Every detail of the different parts of the globe was perfectly depicted on it in paint. The first city name I read was in Borneo, the second was Buenos Aires, the third Alençon. I was dragged away from this game by the sound of a motor. The dirigible skimmed past, just missing me. In the pilots' seats I could see the Captain and Louis Morin.

"I saw your genitals dancing and singing on the savanna!" I shouted at them.

"We made hot air balloons out of them," they replied.

They passed by, but before they had disappeared completely I caught sight of Miss Flowers in the back. She was smoking a cigarette.

Thereupon the wind bore us in opposite directions. A forest of baobabs and palm trees stretched out beneath my feet. The balloon descended slowly. I spied a creole woman on a path. She was crouching down and I couldn't quite make out what she was doing. Through my binoculars I could see her clearly: with her skirts hitched up she was inserting a green snake into her private parts. But the snake was too long. She stood up and, with her skirts still hitched up over her rear, walked off. The snake twisted this way and that like a tail and whistled a lovely little tune that I have since forgotten.

At last the spherical balloon landed. Without delay I hurried after the woman. I soon caught up with her.

"Hello, Desnos," she said.

"How do you know who I am?"

"I once drank cocktails with you and my three cousins at the Taverne de l'Olympia. My brother, the Captain, is a friend of yours."

"What were you doing with that snake?" I asked.

"It's a lovers' game, as well as a children's game. The fruit that opens bit my breasts the night I prostituted myself with a squirrel. But really, this is none of your business."

We continued walking in silence. But after a few minutes I asked her:

"What country is this?"

"The country of demented compasses. Yesterday a boat fell into the tree canopy, we have no idea why. I was brought here by a handsome man with lots of money. But all the men who come here have these strange compasses with two needles."

"Farewell," I said.

She did not reply, but the snake insulted me in the basest terms. Soon they turned off the path. I was alone.

I made my way through the trees towards a small bandstand. A door opened and I walked down a long corridor and then right in to the Pelican Bar. Miss Flowers was seated at the bar on a high stool. I sat down next to her. The barman was speaking. When he saw me he brought out two bottles of kümmel and continued with his story:

"So Minerva followed the war song of the old man with an actual man…"

Two adolescents sat down beside me.

"I'm telling you he is," one of them said to the other.

"Course he is. It's blindingly obvious."

"You think he's sleeping with that American chick?"

"And then some."

*chimney rocket call of the hand bright sunshine that*
*we, what do you want*
*we want the key to the door that opens on to the road*
*we want the road that leads to the countryside*
*we want the countryside that leads to the sea*
*we want the sea that makes the boat dance*
*we want the boat that smokes languidly*
*we want the smoke that takes us to continents*
*we want the continents the skies the boats the smoke*
*the roads the countrysides the seas and we want to kick down the doors.*

The barman pulled out his revolver. "Hands up!" he cried. All the drinkers did as he said. I was the only one to burst out laughing:

"That's not a revolver, it's a severed penis. The man's a eunuch."

The barman didn't move. I reached over and touched him. He put something in his pocket and left. The other characters did the same. Flowers and I found ourselves alone. The passengers from the dirigible came in. There were thirty of them. They jumped gracefully on to the tables, and then on to the counter, and mixed us a cocktail with the following proportions:

| | |
|---|---|
| Kümmel | 1/5 |
| cherry brandy | 1/3 |

| | |
|---|---|
| fino | 2/15 |
| whisky | 2/15 |
| gin | 3/15 |
| angostura XX | drops |
| ice and slices of lemon | |

After which they left without having uttered a single word. True enough though, they didn't have mouths. I put the mysterious compass on the table. The needles were spinning rapidly in opposite directions. The poles were colliding with each other. Large polar bears were clutching boas, and car headlights were chattering:

*The fire moving backwards*
*the sound that emerges from the ear*
*the speech that inflates the stomach*
*the luminous eye*
*these are the characteristics of the master of time and the silver mines.*

Motorists drove their cars ever faster. The sky above Paris was streaked with meteors. Circles of solid fire were spinning in all directions. Some had glowing tails. Lunatic astronomers fell to the moon. Flowers and I stayed quiet. At last the door opened. No one came in. I closed the door. The door opened, again no one came in.

"Let's go," said the American woman.

I pointed out to her that the Big Wheel had been rebuilt. It was turning faster than the wheel of a car. Its axle was gleaming. Above our heads the dirigible was slowly adjusting its course; it was surrounded by a flotilla of aeroplanes and spherical balloons. All of a sudden the balloons burst into flames. They burned with hydrogen's pale and silent fire. Their gondolas fell with a great roar but we could find no trace of them. The planes drifted away in all directions. The dirigible rose straight up. Once it had reached a great height it opened out into a parachute and slowly floated down. Hanging from it was a woman. I recognised her as the woman who had been sodomised by the snake in the baobab forest.

Miss Flowers recognised her too.

"Hello Maud."

"Hello Flowers."

They stripped off their clothes and, paying no more attention to me than to a squadron of dreadnoughts, began to make passionate love. As for me, I watched as torpedo boats collided with floating mines, submarines transformed mighty battleships into great sprays of foam, and aeroplanes bombarded the submersibles. At one point nothing was left of the whole powerful fleet apart from a mast that rose up several metres above the waves. The tricoloured pennant flapped one more time then sank beneath the waves just as the ship had gone down before it.

When I was absolutely sure that the Eiffel Tower had disappeared I made my way to the Champ de Mars. I wasn't mistaken.

For the second time the tower had been swallowed up. In its place was a staircase. I was about to go down when the sound of shouting made me turn round. It was Miss Flowers and Maud.

"Wait for us, wait for us!"

I took them both by the hand and we went down into the underground. On the walls were written several slogans and proverbs:

*If you are looking for death you will find the city.*
*The city you should live in has two ears and a mouth and two eyes.*
*The eyes of miracles always spring from eyes without glasses.*
*Everything becomes tiring and especially meeting people.*
*If you plant wheat, you will reap poppies.*
*A good deed is sometimes useful to someone.*
*What would be extraordinary would be if the extraordinary never occurred.*
*Nothing is gained by running if you don't make love.*
*To the miserly father, a paralysed grandfather.*
*It's easy to lie when seeking your fortune.*
*One often finds oneself in need of a cigarette paper.*
*Ingratitude is cowardice, recognition a swindle.*
*The heart is a bird fit to eat in arithmetic silence.*
*Packets of expensive cigarettes are always empty.*

Miss Flowers read them out aloud. Maud tripped and fell. A steward appeared before us. He was wearing a gold-trimmed cap and a cornflower-blue suit. Vague murmuring from the forests within the conveyor belt that carries the little typist's kisses to far-off continents. In vain, customs officers took aim at the carrier pigeons used by smugglers. The skyscrapers were lit up. Boats coming in to port from the high seas were announcing their arrival, and drunkards acted out their semaphore movements. In their office lit with paraffin lamps, telegraph operators were transcribing the day's news:

"A crime has been committed. A woman, the mother of a small family, has been convicted of stealing a loaf of bread. How? Montéhus will tell you this evening at the Kursaal."*

Once she had read it, Miss Flowers ripped up the telegram the steward had handed to her.

"Come," she said to us.

We hurried over to the Pelican Bar. Behind us, the Eiffel Tower rose up slightly from the ground, out of curiosity.

The room was filled with serious-looking people. All of a sudden cries rang out. Maud had been stabbed and had fallen to the floor. The electricity went off. It came back on again for one second in every ten. People had just enough time to take aim at a nearby face and then throw a punch in the darkness. Blood spurted into their sleeves, into the gap between their shirts and their jackets, all the way up to their elbows. During one flash of light I caught sight of the Captain. He was brandishing a siphon. No shouts disturbed the fighting. Miss Flowers and I were drinking bottomless cocktails. Suddenly the lights came on.

There was no one left in the bar. And all that remained of Maud was one high-heeled suede shoe.

"Miss Flowers," I exclaimed, "let's stop all this joking around."

"You're either crazy or guilty," she replied.

"Come now, take off your masks! The cardinal's nephew is never going to be crucified, nor will any younger siblings be strangled in underground basements. Listen to me: whether the Captain and Louis Morin take turns to be your lovers, or whether Baignoire and Verdure restrict their mathematical concerns of summer nights to the smiles of women, it matters little to me. This shoe is evidence that a serious crime has been committed. Look."

I lifted up the counter. From behind it I brought out two breasts, two legs, two arms, a head (Mado's) and a torso.

"Here is the proof of your power," I said.

"And what now?"

"You are right."

I kissed her on the lips. But she pushed me away.

"Listen," she said.

From the road we could hear the sound of the tide coming in.

The water level was already rising in the bar. We left. The night was clear, the pavements dry. We walked towards our house. Jacques Baron was waiting for us at the door. I told him about Mado's horrible death.

"I didn't know the woman," he said, "but I loved her like a geranium or the anchor of a hot-air balloon. It matters little to me, in the end, if we swear in a woman as president of the Republic. Even the name of your memories offends me. I don't know how to play draughts, or chess, poker or bridge. But, from astride my goitred horse I bet on Europe's fate, and lost. Since then, Vesuvius has spewed out the bellies of black women and the buttocks of Chinese women. Peasants in the fields have abandoned their crops and I spit on their tombs when I come across them. Everywhere I go women kiss me on the forehead. I replaced their sexual organs with an isosceles triangle drawn with chalk on a blackboard. Your full, red lower lip suggests to me very specific lusts. We will never be in love, but I'm willing to try with your help to open up a huge canal between the Indian and Atlantic oceans, cut right across Europe. The sobs of abandoned mistresses have drowned the homosexual dancers from the Pelican Bar in a sea in which they have never learned to swim. The life buoys you owe your survival to are floating behind your heads like halos. There is a scratch on your right elbow and some comet dust on your left knee."

I opened the door. We went inside.

Soldiers surrounded us.

"Go ahead and shoot me if you wish," I said.

We made our way to the Gare Saint-Lazare. A guillotine had been set up there.

"No blindfold. And I want to be guillotined lying on my back so I can see all the other kings who have lain in the machine as they sang of their absurd desires on the backs of calendars."

"As you wish."

The Chinese army formed a guard of honour. Miss Flowers was smoking and laughing. Vitrac and Aragon were playing poker, Breton and Mme Breton were sketching strange profiles of people in charcoal on the white wall of a nearby house. The soldiers laid me down on my back. Benjamin Péret's arm released the mechanism. My horizon was the top beam of the wooden frame. With a jolt, the blade slid down.

Miss Flowers's laugh was grating on my nerves. I pulled my head out of the lunette.* A Chinese soldier grabbed me by the hair to hold my head in position. The blade fell and sliced through his wrist. Benjamin Péret's arm held the severed hand in a tight but friendly grip. Bound by this symbol of friendship they went off together. I ripped out the eyes of the eighty Chinamen who stood around me. They allowed me to do this without saying so much as a word. While I was playing marbles they left, keeping step in ranks of four. They were holding their giant penises in both hands, using them as flagpoles for their colourful standards.

"The flags fluttering from our penises are the symbol of your hymens. Sit there, powerless, on your thrones. Our sexual organs have a sacred perfume, the delicious perfume of erect penises and parted women's thighs. Love yourselves for our flesh and drink our sperm

WHICH GLOWS IN THE DARK."

Vitrac and Aragon, having gambled everything away, were now laying bets on different parts of their bodies. Before long they'd been reduced to a pile of micellaneous limbs that got swept up in a cyclone of Chinese pigtails. I found out these were the bodies that had been torn apart whilst still alive by the helicoidal beings. I grabbed Miss Flowers by the hair.

"The node of the tightly squeezed heart will oxidise the brightness of adventuring footsteps.
Do not tell me the date nor what time it is nor if it is daylight or if it is raining.
Like a water lily deep in Scorpio's thoughts surrounded by burning coal.
I crouch down on the ground. These eyes? I already have a hundred and sixty marbles and now these two as well to play

with on the pavements.

Our heaven which art in father thy breasts be in the mouths of gluttonous fish.

Thine arrival at the Gare de Lyon be unceremonious.

The pinnacle of thy desire know its multiplication tables. And let us fall from the ground into the sky.

Give us this day to our ravening phalluses, our vaginas bursting with desire, the lakes of Tanganyika filled with children's sphincters. And give missals tucked into dictionaries to all those who have the pox."

"Is that it?"

"That's it," she replied.

With great skill I cut off her right breast. Three roads opened up before me. I took the first one. It led to the plaster statue of a man in shirt-sleeves. I shook the man's hand and invited him to dinner but he did not reply. The water that fell from the sky turned him into a milky pulp. The vacant pedestal was overrun with grasshoppers, which rose straight up and disappeared. A milestone pointed in the direction of a town where the smoke from its factories was dribbling on to women's bellies. A man and a young boy were coming towards me from the town. The boy grabbed his father by the neck and strangled him. He pulled his father's head until his neck stretched to a strand as thin as macaroni. With one sharp movement he uncoupled the skull on the right from the body on the left. Jumping up, with his father's neck lying there like a piece of string, he ran off.

I turned back the way I had come. I tore both thighs off the American woman. They ignited spontaneously in my fingers and burned like votive candles. I seized the rest of her body and carried it into the throne-room. I planted it on the phallic seat. Kneeling down, I brought my lips to my mistress's thighs. My teeth bit down on the stalk of some kind of fruit. I tugged. An orange slipped out of her vagina. I squeezed it. It made a noise like the horn of the car that had carried me off to Les Invalides.

I saw that the crypt was all lit up. Stuck together in pairs, like dogs after coitus, the inhabitants of Paris squeezed in. They were singing the Marseillaise. Serious-looking men in their underwear stood weeping tenderly at the chest-high red rope that held them back.

The arena grew even larger. The bull's charge echoed behind me as I ran. The pirates of Tortuga* were lighting a huge fire. A square, the square of the Tour St Jacques, sprang up out of it. I walked down alleyways lined with arches on either side.

"See how I push the sun away so scornfully with my foot. The fuses that explode beneath the bare feet of these women have never proved their love."

The four naked women surrounded me. A deep curtsey bent them in two, so that the tips of their fingers grazed their toes. I stuck some votive candles into these fleshy candelabras.

"Immobilised by my wishes as they are, please look after the remains of Miss Flowers, my beloved mistress. This woman I played with less than I did with red apple compote, or the song of a gosling in a ballroom."

Wax was trickling down their thighs and arms. A repulsive sight! In the barge down by the bridge were piles of gold and silver coins. Anyone who took them quickly decomposed into artichoke fumes.

The Colorado River* flowed round the Marquesas Islands. The sea serpent evaporated.

I got back into the car, but there was a bag on the seat. I opened it. It contained a hundred and sixty-two ocular marbles. I flung them across the street; they turned into electric light-bulbs. A policeman was standing nearby.

"Point me to a street with no lamp-posts or pavements."

"Take the right, the left, or go straight ahead. Fire from the sky will fall on the virgin's belly."

"Where are Baignoire, Verdure, Vitrac, Aragon, Breton and Mme Breton, and the others?"

"I am not acquainted with these people."

With one kick I split his stomach open. Out tumbled stuffing and bran, along with the pearl and diamond necklaces that belonged to Flowers.

Feeling quite appalled by this I searched for somewhere I could take sanctuary. The aquarium at the Trocadéro suited me well. I went inside.

The fish were busily moving about.

At the bottom of one of the tanks I noticed Vitrac's corpse, lying in the arms of a woman. The woman was still alive.

"What a lovely little fish of horizons and geographical maps this woman is," I exclaimed.

She was batrachian, and so beautiful she made all the Vesuviuses melt beneath the footsteps of her lovers.

"What's your name?"

"Suzanne."*

"Would you love me a little, even if it means dying afterwards?"

With a snap of her teeth she pulled a shred of something from Vitrac's belly. A bit of honeysuckle was left sticking to her lips, but out from Vitrac's belly there came a stream of goldfish. They formed themselves into a line and behind this screen Suzanne turned into a blossoming water lily. I picked the beautiful yellow flower and tucked it into my buttonhole. Now eels were slithering out of the belly of my former friend. I left, with Suzanne's perfume, and Suzanne herself, on my clothes.

I got to the Musée Grévin. The waxwork statues of M. and Mme

Breton were seated on a sofa. When I scratched them with my fingernail I realised they were actually their corpses covered with a fine layer of wax. They had little yellow light-bulbs for eyes. When I pressed Breton's stomach a mechanism spoke the words:

"That's clever what you just did."

Outside on the boulevard as I left an empty horse-drawn hearse was passing by. Four undertakers were sitting where the coffin should be, eating saucisson and drinking red wine. The driver had a big rosette pinned to his chest and the bells on the horses' bridles tinkled merrily. Further on, six patisserie chefs in white uniforms went by, pulling a handcart. Each of them was holding a red paper lantern.

I stopped in front of a cinema. Handsome faces smiled out from the posters. I went inside. A bright circle had been projected on to the white screen, but there was no landscape or people.

The audience of empty seats was concentrating on some magnificent spectacle that I could not see.

Infuriated, I had to take a closer look. I climbed up and over the canvas screen. I was blinded by the light of the lantern and then I saw two holes in the screen, large enough for a man to get through. I stuck my head through one of them. A panorama of the city spread out before my eyes. Aragon and Baron had been impaled through their stomachs on two cathedral spires.

I understood that they too had wanted to see what was

happening behind the screen, and the sheer beauty of their suicide was obvious to me.

Leaping from one balcony to the next I made my way back down to the ground.

The streams were planted with watercress where frogs were singing. The cars had only two wheels, one at the front and one at the back. The people were half red and half blue.

A few people were sitting in a circle listening to a concert performed on dynamos and telegraph keys.

The flowerbeds had been replaced by pretty enamelled signs, with beautiful numbers and letters.

On the walls of the houses were reproduced the faces of dominoes and dice.

Large herons, attached to the ground by hundred-metre lengths of silk thread tied to their feet, were flying around the Tour St Jacques. I didn't know what sort of expression I should assume.

The colour of the flags had changed. They were made of asbestos, the flagpoles of nickel. The motto BATHHOUSE, inexplicable, was etched into their folds.

The soldiers who were carrying them were eating macaroni, morsels of which dangled from the corners of their mouths. Some fell off. Children fought to see who could gobble up these scraps of food all mixed up with horse droppings and engine oil.

THIS IS THE CEMETERY
OF THE PASSENGERS OF
*LA SÉMILLANTE*
LOST AT SEA
ITS BODIES AND CHATTELS
WRECKED ON THE REEFS
OF THE ILES SANGUINAIRES.

| *here lies* | *here lies* | *here lies* | *here lies* | *here lies* |
|---|---|---|---|---|
| André Breton | Simone Breton | Louis Aragon | Jacques Baron | René Crevel |
| *here lies* Max Morise | *here lies* Drieu la Rochelle | *here lies* Philippe Soupault | *here lies* Georges Auric | *here lies* Roger Vitrac |
| *here lies* Miss Flowers | *here lies* Robert Desnos | *here lies* Georges Limbour | *here lies* Francis Picabia | *here lies* Jules Mary |
| *here lies* Baignoire | | | | *here lies* G.R.D. |

COMMON GRAVE

*here lie*

Isidore Ducasse   Arthur Rimbaud
Alfred Jarry   Guillaume Apollinaire
Jacques Vaché   Gérard de Nerval
Eugène Sue   Baudelaire
Germain Nouveau
and others

| *here lies* Verdure | | *here lies* Pablo Picasso |
|---|---|---|
| *here lies* Paul Eluard | | *here lies* Giorgio de Chirico |
| *here lies* Benjamin Péret | | *here lies* Derain |

| *here lies* | *here lie* | *here lies* | *here lies* | *here lies* |
|---|---|---|---|---|
| Tristan Tzara | The two Josephsons | Suzanne de L. de K. | Théodore Fraenkel | Georges Braque |
| *here lies* Nazimova | *here lies* God | *here lies* Mirette Maîtrejean | *here lies* Gustave Aimard | *here lies* Someone |
| *here lies* May Woodson | *here lies* Robespierre | *here lies* Reverdy | *here lies* Archduke Rudolf of Hapsburg | *here lies* The balloonist André |

A two-sou coin fell to the ground. At last I was going to find out what I should do. Life or suicide, either was pointless. Heads or tails. I flipped the coin up in the air. It turned into a marine sextant that rose into the sky with the sound of hundreds of birds flapping their wings. I watched its ascent.

> *Glory to the judge's foppish circle*
> *Justice will at last their heads encircle*
> *Behold their feet their fingers and their hair*
> *so too my lip, my lower lip, and stare.*

Fatal recklessness! My words floated up into the atmosphere. They stuck to the sextant and paralysed it. It fell with the whistling sound torpedoes make. It hit me on the back of the head and scattered my dust over the twenty-three shores of seventeen continents, with a terrible noise that reproduced exactly this syllable: *PING!*

## THE END

## TRANSLATOR'S NOTES
(Unless indicated otherwise)

Page 34. What's the use of pulling the cord? [Author's note]

37. The Taverne de l'Olympia was a restaurant, on the corner of the Boulevard des Capucines and the Rue Caumartin, presumably so called because of its proximity to the Olympia music hall, and in a part of Paris associated at the time with prostitution. It was a favourite haunt of the dancer Rachel in books 2 and 3 of Proust's *A la recherche du temps perdu.*

38. *Baignoire* = Bathtub.

38. *Verdure* = Greenery, or Salad.

38. The Magdeburg Hemispheres, originally made of copper, were used to demonstrate the power of atmospheric pressure: when fitted together with an airtight seal the air could be pumped out, leaving a vacuum inside. Teams of horses could not pull the halves apart. The experiment was designed by the 17th-century German scientist and mayor of Magdeburg, Otto von Guericke, to demonstrate the air pump he had recently invented.

45. A *porte cochère* is a porch-like structure at the entrance to a building through which a horse and carriage can pass in order for the occupants to alight under cover, protected from the weather.

53. The formula for finding the solutions of a general quadratic equation ($ax^2 + bx + c = 0$), as occurs later in the text, on p.92. [CA]

61. A hereditary noble ruler of a town or castle and the surrounding area.

68. An aromatised wine that was infused with the bark of the cinchona tree, the source of quinine.

69. I.e. the walrus.

86. In English in the original.

90. A fearsome monster that lived in Provence, with a dragon's body, a hard, spiked shell on its back and a whip-like tail.

98. Ys, a city of Celtic myth on the coast of Brittany, was believed to be the most magnificent city in the world, but was overtaken by sin and eventually swallowed up by a huge wave.

111. Spanish in the original, a drove of cattle.

129. A café-concert hall on the Avenue de Clichy in Paris.

133. The part of the guillotine that holds the head still as the blade comes down.

135. Tortuga is an island in the Caribbean, so named by Christopher Columbus because he thought it resembled a turtle shell rising out of the sea. It was famous as a haven for Caribbean pirates in the 17th and 18th centuries.

136. The Rio Colorado, in southern Argentina.

137. Perhaps Suzanne, the first love of Roger Vitrac, and whom Desnos certainly knew in 1922. Or possibly the Suzanne in the cemeteries, unless they are one and the same.

*APPENDICES*

*Appendix I: A Second Cemetery*

The second manuscript of *The Punishments of Hell* contains a different version of the cemetery.

*here lies*
Louis
Aragon

*here lies*
Jacques
Baron

*here lies*
André
Breton

*here lies*
Philippe
Soupault

*here lies*
Max
Morise

*here lies*
Robert
Desnos

*here lies*
Francis
Picabia

*here lies*
Simone
Breton

*here lies*
Paul
Eluard

*here lies*
Miss
Flowers

*here lies*
Marcel
Duchamp

*here lies*
Germaine
Everling

*here lies*
Benjamin
Péret

*here lies*
Drieu la
Rochelle

COMMON GRAVE
*here lie*

*here lies*
Georges
Auric

Isidore Ducasse   Baudelaire   Robespierre

*here lies*
Georges
Limbour

Gustave Aimard   Arthur Rimbaud
Germain Nouveau   St Just

*here lies*
Pierre
de Massot

*here lies*
Théodore
Fraenkel

Alexandre Dumas *le père*   Alfred Jarry
Pierre Souvestre and Marcel Allain
Jacques Vaché   Gérard de Nerval

*here lies*
Max
Ernst

*here lies*
Louis de
Gonzague-
Frick

Eugène Sue
and various others

*here lies*
Giorgio de
Chirico

*here lies*
Mirette
Maîtrejean

*here lies*
Verdure

*here lies*
Baignoire

*here lies*
E. and L. de
Kermadec

*here lies*
God

*here lies*
Nazimova

*here lies*
May
Wilson

*here lies*
Jim Mac
Kinley

*here lies*
Paul
Smara

*here lies*
Pierre
Reverdy

*here lies*
Jean
Horth

*here lies*
The balloonist
André

*here lies*
Roger
Vitrac

*here lies*
Suzanne de
L. de K.

*here lies*
G.R.D.

*Appendix II: Letter from Robert Desnos to Jacques Doucet*

Paris, 22 October 1922

Sir,

André Breton has told me of your intentions regarding the manuscript of *New Hebrides* and I am deeply flattered. I fear, however, that my natural awkwardness may hamper my ability to express quite how much this has affected me.

This is my first work of prose, and I wrote it with no other purpose than to amuse myself, eager as I was to fill the void in which I found myself at the beginning of the year. I had just returned from Morocco, having spent fourteen fairly brutal months cut off from most of the things that used to make me happy. I had just made the acquaintance of Aragon and Breton and naturally they both became characters in the sort of stories I have enjoyed making up for as long as I can remember. These are the stories that fill my hours of solitude, usually before I fall asleep, lingering on into my dreams and serving as a sort of preface to them. *New Hebrides* is simply the direct writing down of one of these stories naturally commingled with the transcription of the dreams that may have been triggered by it. I have done my best to evoke the friendship (amongst other feelings) that some of them can inspire in me. I have followed no particular plan, nor have I had any concern for either artistry or plausibility, while the freedom of the writing is no more than what occurs in private thoughts and dreams.

I wrote the first page one idle evening at the Petit Grillon café, in the Passage des Panoramas, while I was waiting for one of the main characters in the novel to turn up. I carried on after that wherever I was, in cafés (particularly a small bar on the Ile de la Cité which was popular with bargemen), on the train, in my room or at the office where I work.

The start of the work was marked by a coincidence that while undoubtedly trivial was nevertheless entertaining in its way. It so happened that André Breton had fixed a blackboard to his door and, unaware of this, I informed him that something had been scribbled on his door.

I think in the main I have been influenced by *The Poet Assassinated*, and, for the supernaturalistic part, *The Magnetic Fields*.

But perhaps I have said too much about me and my *New Hebrides*, and should apologise for having the vanity to make any comparison between it and the works written by those friends of mine who appear in it, and compared with whom I am altogether lacking in firepower. Please accept my thanks for showing such an interest in my early efforts and I sincerely hope both that my intentions have not been presumptuous and that there may be found in these pages perhaps a little something beyond what I wrote there. It is to be published this winter, with a frontispiece by Francis Picabia. Please excuse the rambling nature of this letter, but Breton will tell you how certain recent experiences have managed to change me and make me lose certain notions of polite behaviour.

I remain, sir, your obedient servant,
    Robert Desnos

*Appendix III: Biographies*

Gustave Aimard (1818–1883). Prolific author of children's adventure stories (see Introduction).

The "Balloonist André": André-Jacques Garnerin (1769–1823). Also the first person to make a parachute jump.

Guillaume Apollinaire (1880–1918). Arguably the greatest French poet of early modernism, friend of Picasso, Jacob, Jarry etc., who died from a combination of war wounds and influenza.

Louis Aragon (1897–1982). Poet and novelist and one of the leading figures in the French Dadaist and Surrealist movements. Atlas publishes his first novel, *Anicet or the Panorama* (see p.159).

Georges Auric (1899–1983). Avant-garde composer and member of the group Les Six, with Satie and Poulenc, at the time this book was written.

Jacques Baron (1905–1986). French poet and Surrealist writer.

Maurice Barrès (1862–1923). Novelist, journalist and politician who is considered one of the main promoters of nationalism at the turn of the century in France. In spring 1921 the Dadaists organised his trial *in absentia*, charging him with an "attack on the security of the mind", and sentencing him to 20 years' forced labour.

Georges Braque (1882–1963). The other major Cubist painter, with Picasso.

André Breton (1896–1966). Founder of the Dadaist movement in France, and then of Surrealism. His *Surrealist Manifesto* of 1924 defined Surrealism as "pure psychic automatism", as practised before the fact by Robert Desnos.

Simone Breton (1897–1980). The first of André Breton's three wives. They divorced in 1929.

François Sadi Carnot (1837–1894). The fifth president of the Third Republic, from 1887 until he was assassinated in 1894.

René Crevel (1900–1935). Writer active in both Dadaism and Surrealism. During the so-called "Period of Sleeping-Fits", he and Desnos were the most impressive "performers", able to fall into a trance at will and produce reams of complex texts.

Robert Delaunay (1885–1941). "Orphist" artist, famous for his semi-abstract depictions of the Eiffel Tower.

André Derain (1880–1954). One of the *fauves* group of painters.

Paul Déroulède (1846–1914). Right-wing author and politician, one of the founders of the nationalist League of Patriots.

Pierre Drieu la Rochelle (1893–1945). Novelist and essayist (later a fascist and Nazi collaborator) who was close to the Dadaists at the time Desnos was writing *The Punishments of Hell.*

Ducasse, see Lautréamont.

Marcel Duchamp (1887–1968). Then a rather unknown artist whose pseudonym, Rrose Sélavy, Desnos would channel during the Surrealist *"sommeils"*.

Alexandre Dumas *le père* (1802–1870). Prolific author, best known for *The Three Musketeers* and *The Count of Monte Cristo*.

Paul Eluard (1895–1952). Close associate of Breton, Aragon and Soupault, and perhaps the greatest poet of French Surrealism.

Germaine Everling (1886-1976). Partner of Francis Picabia at the time this book was written.

Théodore Fraenkel (1896–1964). A close friend of Desnos who was involved with Dada in Paris and then early Surrealism. He later became a doctor.

Francis I (1494–1547). The first king of France.

The Goncourt brothers, Edmond (1822–1896) and Jules (1830–1870). French writers and diarists whose estate funds the Prix Goncourt, probably the most important literary prize in French literature.

Louis de Gonzague-Frick (1883–1959). A poet and literary critic, involved in various 20th-century avant-garde movements. A close friend of Apollinaire and of Desnos.

Maréchal de Gramont, Antoine III Agénor de Gramont (1604–1678). A French military man and diplomat, who served as Marshal of France from 1641.

G.R.D. i.e. Georges Ribemont-Dessaignes (1884–1974). Key early participant in the Paris Dada movement, notably in works for theatre and music. Later associated with the Surrealists until becoming disaffected with the movement in 1929 (along with Desnos).

Louis Lazare Hoche (1768–1797). French soldier who became a general of the Revolutionary army.

Jean Horth, unknown.

Victor Hugo (1802–1885). Poet, novelist and dramatist of "high" Romanticism, a Surrealist when he wasn't stupid, according to Breton.

Isabeau of Bavaria (1371–1435). Eldest daughter of Duke Stephen III of Bavaria-Ingolstadt and Taddea Visconti of Milan who became Queen of France when she married King Charles VI in 1385.

Alfred Jarry (1873–1907). Writer best known for his play *Ubu Roi* (1896), who coined the term and philosophical concept of 'Pataphysics. He was championed by both the Dadaists and Surrealists at a time when it seemed he might be forgotten.

Matthew Josephson (1899–1978) and his wife Hannah (1900–1976) were involved in the Paris Dada Group in its earliest days. They later worked in journalism and literary criticism.

Eugène de Kermadec (1899–1976). Painter, who later showed at the Galerie Louise Leiris. His wife was called Lucette.

Suzanne de L. de K., presumably a relative of the painter de Kermadec (previous entry), possibly the "Suzanne" mentioned in the text.

The Comte de Lautréamont was the pseudonym of Isidore-Lucien Ducasse (1846–1870), Uruguayan-born author of *Les Chants de Maldoror* and

*Poésies*, major influences on modern French literature.

Georges Limbour (1900–1970). Writer and early member of the Surrealist group, later associated with Georges Bataille and then the Collège de 'Pataphysique.

Jim Mac Kinley, unknown.

Rirette Maîtrejean, pseudonym of Anna Estorges (1887–1968). A militant anarchist and champion of free love, connected to the Bonnot Gang.

Georges Malkine (1898–1970). Painter, writer, illustrator and actor who first met Desnos in 1922; the pair immediately became great friends.

Marengo (*c.*1793-1831). Napoleon's horse, named after the battle of the same name (14 June 1800), fought between French forces under Bonaparte and Austrian forces near the city of Alessandria, in Piedmont.

Jules Mary (1851–1922). French popular novelist, a school-friend of Rimbaud.

Pierre de Massot (1900–1969). Active in Paris Dada, he wrote the first history of the movement.

Gaston Montéhus, pseudonym of Gaston Mardochée Brunswick (1872–1952). A French singer-songwriter.

Louis Morin (1855–1938). Prolific book illustrator, his commissions ranged from literary to children's books to "curiosa".

Max Morise (1900–1973). Surrealist artist and translator, a friend of both Desnos and Vitrac.

Alla Nazimova (1879–1945). Russian actress who starred in several

Hollywood films, particularly in the 1920s.

Gérard de Nerval (1808–1855). Key Romantic poet and writer, certain of whose texts, especially *Aurelia*, were highly valued by the Surrealists.

Alfred Nobel (1833–1896). Swedish chemist, inventor, businessman, and philanthropist who bequeathed his fortune to finance the various Nobel Prizes.

Germain Nouveau (1851–1920). Symbolist poet and companion of Rimbaud who travelled widely and spent much of his life in penury.

Benjamin Péret (1899–1959). Dadaist and then one of the central members of the Surrealist movement.

Francis Picabia (1879–1953). Artist and pivotal figure in the international Dada movement owing to his review *391*, which was published from whatever city he happened to be in at the time.

Raymond Poincaré (1860–1934). Conservative statesman who was prime minister of France on three occasions, and president from 1913 to 1920.

Pierre Reverdy (1889–1960). Poet of early modernism, his verse and magazine *Nord-Sud* (co-founded with Apollinaire) were influential on both Dada and Surrealism.

Maximilien Robespierre (1758–1794). Lawyer, politician and member of the Committee of Public Safety during the Terror in Revolutionary France.

Archduke Rudolf of Habsburg (1858–1889). Crown Prince of Austria-Hungary who died with his mistress in a suicide pact at his hunting lodge in Mayerling, an act the Surrealists would later categorise as an example of *"l'amour fou"*.

Saint-Just (1767–1794). The youngest and most ruthless member of the Committee of Public Safety during the Revolution. Guillotined with Robespierre on 9 Thermidor.

Sir Ernest Shackleton (1874–1922). Polar explorer who led three British expeditions to the Antarctic. His Trans-Antarctic Expedition of 1914-17 ended in catastrophe when his ship *Endurance* was trapped in the ice-pack and slowly crushed.

Paul Smara, probably the pseudonym of the French artist Paul Dubois who specialised in explicit homosexual drawings. His dates are unknown, apart from the approximate date of his death (*c.*1980).

Philippe Soupault (1897–1990). Poet, novelist and critic active in the Dada and Surrealist movements, and co-founder, with Breton and Aragon, of the review *Littérature*.

Pierre Souvestre (1874–1914) and Marcel Allain (1885–1969), joint authors of the Fantômas novels.

Eugène Sue (1804–1857). Socialist and anti-Catholic writer and author of serialised novels, most famous for his much-imitated and highly popular *The Mysteries of Paris* of 1842–3.

Tristan Tzara (1896–1963). Romanian-born poet, essayist and performer, co-founder and chief publicist of the Dada movement.

Jacques Vaché (1895–1919). A monocle-wearing opium addict of whom Breton said, "In literature, I was in turn taken with Rimbaud, Jarry,

Apollinaire, Nouveau and Lautréamont, but it is to Jacques Vaché that I owe the most."

Roger Vitrac (1899–1952). Surrealist playwright and poet, who collaborated with Artaud in his Théâtre Alfred Jarry.

May Wilson, probably Edna Mae Wilson (1880–1960), an American silent film actress who starred in about 15 films between 1913 and 1920.

May Woodson, unknown, May Wilson (above) being possibly intended.

# RELATED TITLE

*Anicet or the Panorama*
A Dadaist novel by Louis Aragon
208 pp., 195 x 175 mm., hardback with printed paper case.

Exactly contemporary with *The Punishments of Hell*, this novel, much of it written amidst the horror of the. trenches when Aragon was a medical orderly during the First World War, demonstrates the chasm that separates the works of the artists and writers of what would become Dadaism and those, say, of the English War poets.

In a world of moral destitution beyond any rational forbearance, what can remain? How can one write at all, let alone something as absurd as a novel? *Anicet or the Panorama* is both a *roman à clef* (Aragon's friends, including André Breton, are recognisable), and a novel of the total liquidation of a culture that had allowed this to come to pass: even literary heroes must be confronted and superseded. As fast-paced, funny and surprising as a Hollywood silent movie, its narrative of fabulous crimes and scandals sweeps through a panorama of Paris society as its protagonist Anicet becomes subordinated to the mysterious Mire, a woman who is the incarnation of "modern Beauty". Anicet is seduced into a life of crime, which he accepts with nonchalance and an ironic integrity that he maintains to the bitter end of his journey of self-immolation.

Aragon's precisely crafted and sardonic prose reveals a world that is no more than a tragic puppet show, with every scene self-evidently staged. This furious tempest of a book launched Aragon's career and is one the cornerstones of the Paris Dada movement. It is not at all unreasonable to consider it his greatest work.

ATLAS PRESS *Eclectics & Heteroclites*

For a complete listing of all titles available from Atlas Press and the
London Institute of 'Pataphysics see our o99nline catalogue at:
www.atlaspress.co.uk
To receive automatic notification of new publications
sign on to the emailing list.
Atlas Press, 27 Old Gloucester st., London WC1N 3XX
Trade distribution UK: www.turnaround-uk.com; USA: www.artbook.com